BEGINNER UNDER THE BACKBOARDS

Sports Books by C. Paul Jackson

For younger boys:

BIG PLAY IN THE SMALL LEAGUE
CHRIS PLAYS SMALL FRY FOOTBALL
ERIC AND DUD'S FOOTBALL BARGAIN
FIFTH INNING FADE-OUT
LITTLE LEAGUE TOURNAMENT
LITTLE MAJOR LEAGUER
PEE WEE COOK OF THE MIDGET LEAGUE
STEPLADDER STEVE PLAYS BASKETBALL
TIM, THE FOOTBALL NUT
TOM MOSELY—MIDGET LEAGUER
TOMMY, SOAP BOX DERBY CHAMPION
TWO BOYS AND A SOAP BOX DERBY

For older boys:

BASEBALL'S SHRINE
BUD BAKER, COLLEGE PITCHER
BUD BAKER, HIGH SCHOOL PITCHER
BUD BAKER, RACING SWIMMER
BUD PLAYS JUNIOR HIGH BASKETBALL
BUD PLAYS JUNIOR HIGH FOOTBALL
BUD PLAYS SENIOR HIGH BASKETBALL
BULLPEN BARGAIN
FULLBACK IN THE LARGE FRY LEAGUE
HALFBACK!
HALL OF FAME FLANKERBACK
JUNIOR HIGH FREESTYLE SWIMMER
PASS RECEIVER
PENNANT STRETCH DRIVE
MINOR LEAGUE SHORTSTOP
PRO FOOTBALL ROOKIE
PRO HOCKEY COMEBACK
ROOKIE CATCHER WITH THE ATLANTA BRAVES
ROSE BOWL PRO
SECOND TIME AROUND ROOKIE
SUPER MODIFIED DRIVER
WORLD SERIES ROOKIE

BEGINNER UNDER THE BACKBOARDS

by **C. PAUL JACKSON**

Illustrated by Ned Butterfield

HASTINGS HOUSE · PUBLISHERS, *New York*

LIBRARY OF CONGRESS CATALOGING IN PUBLICATION DATA

Jackson, Caary Paul, 1902–
  Beginner under the backboards.

  SUMMARY: Nearly six feet five inches, a skinny and
uncoordinated fourteen-year-old joins the basketball
beginner's squad and finds he has some unsuspected talents.
  [1. Basketball—Fiction] I. Butterfield, Ned,
illus. II. Title.
PZ7.J1322Be   [Fic]   74-13428
ISBN 0-8038-0762-7

Published simultaneously in Canada by
Saunders of Toronto, Ltd., Don Mills, Ontario

Printed in the United States of America

☐ *CONTENTS*

For Christopher Caary Soudek,
  latest member of the Jackson clan

CHAPTER ONE

□ *THE PROPER SPIRIT*

HE SPRAWLED across five rows of the bleacher seats, a little to the side of other boys in basketball gear. Long legs stuck way out from green shorts; long arms stretched from a green gym shirt. Small letters DSS were sewed in gold thread near the neck opening.

A shock of shiny black hair fell across his forehead as Durand Stanislaus Salvatore shook his head at the action out on the basketball court in Lincoln Junior High gymnasium. Awe filled his wide-set brown eyes. Five boys dressed in gym shirts and basketball pants tore up and down the court against five boys wearing no shirts.

"Stay with him, Olson! He's your man! . . . Long pass. Heave that thing! . . . Up after the rebound! Use your height! . . . It's as much yours as his; give him a battle for the ball! . . ."

Passing the ball. Dribbling. Maneuvering for position. Shooting at the basket. Scrambling for the rebound when a shot missed. Yells from the boys. Comments and advice from the stockily built man in khaki trousers and gray sweatshirt.

COACH was lettered across the front of the sweatshirt. The man's hair was moderately short. Eyes the color of slate seemed to see everything that happened. A whistle dangled from a thong around his neck. The long-legged boy in the bleacher shifted position while he peered at the head man of Lincoln Junior High Basketball.

Coach Raymond J. Long, the guy that Ron Walker built up so that I pulled the fool stunt of coming here, Salvatore thought, like I was in my right mind which for sure I was NOT!

Doggone that Ron! Okay, so he was trying to help out a new guy in the neighborhood. But he sure—oh, heck! No point in blaming Ron Walker—

A wild pass from across the basketball court hit the bottom row of bleacher seats and bounced high toward Salvatore. He reached up a long arm, plucked the ball out of the air and half-pushed the sphere back on the court. A boy with no shirt took the ball out of bounds and whipped a pass to another shirtless player.

The receiver of the pass in bounds took a shot from outside the free-throw circle and missed. The tallest, huskiest boy on the court barged in and leaped high to grab the rebound. Then he dribbled twice, pivoted and pushed the ball gently against the backboard above the steel hoop. The sphere slanted down through the basket cording.

Coach Long shrilled his whistle. "Nice going, Arnold," he said. "All right, forwards and guards of the Skins take a break. Jones, Brown, Olson and Smith peel your shirts and move in at forwards and guards for Butch Arnold's team."

He called four more names. A quartet of boys eagerly came from the bleachers and joined the Shirts. One of the new players took the ball outside beneath the basket. Coach Long again blew his whistle and action resumed.

Butch Arnold continued to dominate rebounds from both backboards. But the general play seemed no different than before the changes, as far as the long-legged boy in the bleachers could see. All these guys are good, he thought. The way they fire passes and dribble and shoot! How could an awkward bozo like me do any good out there? How come I'm here, anyhow?

Heck, I got carried away by what Ron Walker said, that was all. That crazy business about what a great basketball player I'd make and Lincoln spirit and the stuff in the newspaper and—Durand Stanislaus Salvatore was suddenly recalling things Ron had written in the piece he'd shown him.

Mr. Raymond J. Long and Lincoln Junior High are almost basketball twins. He graduated from Western State the year that the our building was completed and Lincoln enrolled its first student body. A three-year star guard on Western's basketball team, Long was drafted by a pro team, but he chose to teach at Lincoln Junior High and coach.

Fair to everybody, varsity squad or the lowly Neversweats, Coach Long is always sympathetic to Lincoln boys' problems on or off the basketball court. He builds confidence because he has absolute confidence in—

A whistle blast cut through Durand Salvatore's mental exercise. "I keep yelling at you fellows to use your height, that the ball belongs to everybody," Coach Long exhorted. "You've got to battle for possession. Sure, I know Arnold is taller than any of you. Okay. You think there won't be big boys on other teams? You have to battle the big guys that much harder!"

The words stopped registering on Salvatore as Coach Long took one boy by the shoulders and talked earnestly to him.

Thing to do is forget the con job Ron Walker gave me. There's no way I could—

"You in the green outfit! Come out here!"

For a moment the long-legged boy did not comprehend the call from the coach. Then he saw other boys looking at him and abruptly realized that he was the only one in green pants and shirt. Unfolding what seemed like yards of legs, he hoisted his loose-jointed, six-foot-four-inch frame and ambled out on the court. He seemed mostly elbows and knees and skinny shanks. Coach Long gazed upward to the freckled face.

"There's no doubt you are tall enough to be a basketball player," the coach said. "You a bonifide Lincoln student?"

"For sure he's bony enough!"

Butch Arnold started to laugh at his own wise crack. Coach Long said, "All right!" Arnold's laugh choked off. The stocky man turned to the tall boy and asked, "Are you enrolled in Lincoln Junior High?"

"Yes, sir. I'm in ninth grade. We moved here last month."

"Your name?"

"Salvatore, sir—Durand Salvatore." Freckles suddenly rippled as he grinned. "But sooner or later it'll be Slats—or maybe Slimjim or Stringbean. Always has."

Snorts of laughter came from the boys. The dry, doleful tone made even Coach Long smile. "Okay then, Slats." Long accepted the self-conviction. "We're interested more in your ability to handle a basketball than your nickname. Height, used to get rebounds, to outjump the other team's men, is essential to gain possession of the ball. Get in here at center for the Shirts."

Slats Salvatore was no match for Butch Arnold's bulk but he was three inches taller. They crouched and tensed for the jump. Coach Long tossed the ball high between the tall boys.

Salvatore seemed to explode upward. He uncoiled and shot into the air. A big hand stretched inches above Arnold's and slapped the ball. But the explosion did not end there. Slats came down with gangling arms flailing like a windmill. A hand raked across Arnold's face. Coach Long shrilled his whistle.

Butch Arnold grabbed at one eye and glared at Slats from the other. "What do you think you're doing," he yelled. "You clumsy jerk!"

He indicated the gold DSS sewed on the taller boy's shirt. "They stand for Dumb Saps School, huh!"

"Nope. Darn Sharp Scuffler." Slats was amazed at his own words.

He smoothed a big hand through disheveled black hair and gulped to the coach, "I'm real sorry if I did something wrong, sir. I thought you wanted me to get to the ball first."

13

Coach Long eyed him narrowly as though wondering if this was a put-on like the DSS explanation. "That is the general idea," he said dryly. "Officials allow a lot of leeway, but the rules still make basketball a no-contact game. Fouling always costs your team possession of the ball, opportunity to gain possession, or maybe points. All right, Arnold. We'll give you a free throw."

Butch Arnold must have known that his free throw try was going to miss. He barreled into the foul lane almost as the ball left his hand. He banged into Slats, hard, as both went after the rebound. But it was Slats who came down with the ball. Long's whistle blasted.

"That is flagrant charging, Arnold!"

"You keep yelling at us that the ball is ours as much as—"

"No beefing," the coach interrupted. "You know very well that leaving the line before the ball hits the basket or backboard is a violation. It would have been the other team's ball out of bounds, if you hadn't fouled. Get-even tactics contribute nothing to anyone's play. Salvatore, you take a free throw."

Slats wondered if the trembling unsureness he felt inside showed as he toed the free throw line. Well, dilly-dallying around would only make his shakiness worse. He eyed the basket. His knees bent; his big hands lofted the ball in a gentle arc. The basketball dropped through the netting without touching rim or backboard.

One of the Skins threw the ball inbounds to Butch Arnold. The husky lad dribbled across the center line then fired a pass to a teammate. Another pass. A Shirts player crowded the boy with the ball and fell victim to a fine head fake. A jump shot arched toward the basket.

The ball bounced off the front of the steel ring. Butch Arnold drove in for the rebound, and abruptly tangled with Slats again. A bony knee whammed against Arnold's thigh; a bony elbow dug into his ribs. One hand belted Arnold's neck as Slats tipped the ball with the other. When they landed, Slats clutched the ball firmly with both hands.

Again the coach blasted his whistle shrilly. He eyed Slats Salvatore. "That's another foul," Long said. "Just where did you learn to play basketball?"

"Why—why—I—" A frown made Slats' freckles ripple. "I guess you couldn't rightly say I *have* learned to play basketball," he said. "They didn't have a gym or a team where I went to school."

The coach continued to eye him. "You sunk that free throw as smooth as a veteran," Long said.

"We did have a rickety basket fastened to a pole, sir. No backboard, we had to drop the ball through the ring. Sometimes, I was pretty good tossing underhand with both hands."

Slats sighed, dropped his eyes to the floor then looked at the coach.

"I know I don't measure up," Slats said.

"It was a crazy thing to do to come over here. I won't be bothering you again. I—I guess I'd better—"

"Hold up." Coach Long broke in. "Why *did* you—ah—come over here, as you put it?"

"Well, the boy across the street where we moved kept telling me I needed to—you see, sir, he wants to be a sports writer. Maybe you know him. Ron Walker?"

Long nodded, said, "Walker interviewed me for a piece he's doing for the Kid Sports Page of *CITY NEWS*. What does he have to do with you trying out for our basketball team?"

"Well, I read his material. How you're fair and even help kids who aren't so good with the Neversweats and all. Ron said I'd be crazy not to try out with my height and I just need confidence and you'd help and how I ought to get the right Lincoln spirit and—"

Slats Salvatore's voice trailed off. The coach nodded after a moment.

"We certainly can use all the height we can get," he said. "And you have the proper spirit. Maybe we can help you. But perhaps your—ah—talents had better be developed on the Neversweats for a while."

CHAPTER TWO

□ RIGHT NAMES—WRONG NAMES

"U-m-m-m! Man, is that ever good!"

Ron Walker eyed the flaky, golden pastry he held in one hand. Sweet, rich filling oozed from two large bites. He pushed the crosspiece of his glasses higher on his nose. Real appreciation was in Ron's blue eyes as he looked from the pastry to Slats Salvatore.

"I've never tasted anything so luscious," Ron said. "Roll-cake, you call it? This filling is really something! What's it made of?"

"Dates and nuts and honey and spices and I don't know what all," Slats said.

A wire basket was fastened to the handlebars of the bicycle his long legs straddled. A metal lunch box was in the basket. One hand steadied the handlebars while Slats popped the final piece of his roll-cake into his mouth. He chewed briefly, swallowed and licked a bit of filling from his thumb.

"It's a recipe handed down from Dad's ancestors in Italy," Slats went on. "He likes two roll-cakes in his lunch. The batch Mom had in the oven wasn't ready when he left, so I'm taking his lunch to him."

Slats inclined his head toward the metal container in the bike basket. "I sure wish Dad didn't work nights, even if it was the promotion that brought us here."

Ron smacked his lips after the last of his delicacy was swallowed. He said, "I don't blame him for wanting two. Be sure and tell your mother how much I liked the roll-cake she sent me."

"I won't have a chance to forget. First thing Mom will want to know is whether her bribe worked."

Ron jerked his head up to look at Slats. A shock of almost-white blond hair jounced over his forehead and Ron brushed it back. The puzzlement in his tone was matched by his expression when Ron asked, "Did you say bribe?"

"What else?" Slats grinned. "I told Mom about the name stuff you put out to me. So, she wants you to look up her given name, and Dad's, in your *Names Are Names* booklet."

"I don't carry the thing around in my pocket. Come on in and we'll see if they are in the booklet."

"Huh-uh." Slats shook his head. "I have to get going. Kind of funny, I was surprised Mom was interested in the name stuff. And I sort of wonder what Coach Long meant by the Neversweats. That be in *Names Are Names?*"

"It only gives meanings of real names," Ron said. "But Neversweats is the name somebody thought up for the guys Coach works with nights after supper. They're kids who want to play basketball but aren't good enough to make the varsity squad. They don't have to sweat winning the way the varsity does."

"Yeah. Well, he said I'd better report to the Neversweats, after I just about wrecked the practice scrimmage. I was going to—"

"There you go again!" Ron interrupted. He pushed at his glasses. "The way I heard it, what you wrecked was Butch Arnold more'n practice! Will you get it through your thick head that bad-mouthing yourself is no good!"

Slats said nothing. Ron went on. "I'll bet Coach was glad to see old Butch cut down to size!"

"Sounds like you aren't exactly one of Arnold's big boosters."

Ron frowned, then pushed the crosspiece of his glasses.

"Butch Arnold has been the big man too long," he said. "Could be I'm sort of prejudiced because I'm pulling so hard for you to get confidence in Slats Salvatore. How do you feel about Butch?"

"Well, I guess I'd have to say he got under my skin some." Slats looked thoughtful. "Not that he bugged me so bad I want to knock him around, or anything. He sure can play basketball! Look, I wrote out Mom's and Dad's names. I'll leave the paper and pick it up on the way back to the gym."

Ron read aloud from the paper Slats handed him. "Enrico and Ludmilla Nada. Unusual names."

"Dad's is a longtime name in his family way back in Italy, and Mom's folks came from Czech farming country." Slats put one foot on a bike pedal, then said, "Hey! I've been going to ask you what Ronald Walker means!"

Ron chuckled. His eyes sparkled. "I wondered when you'd get around to that. Walker isn't in *Names Are Names*. It probably just means 'one who walks'. Ronald is of Teutonic origin. It means"—Ron pushed his glasses higher on his nose and grinned—"powerful judgment."

Ron's chuckle became full-throated laughter. "That's why I accept whatever the booklet gives as right on the ball!" he added.

Coach Raymond Long chucked a basketball from hand to hand while he eyed the group of boys in basketball gear. Slats looked around. He stood head and shoulders above anyone else in the group.

Sure a creepy-looking bunch, he thought. Would-be basketball players. They all looked as though they felt as unnecessary as he did. Neversweats, huh? No sweat, all right, as far as ever getting beyond the would-be class.

"No boy will ever be cut from the Neversweats." Coach Long began his opening talk. "However, it is probable that some of you may discover after a workout or two that you simply do not yet have the physical capabilities, the coordination and stamina to play basketball.

"You may drop out at anytime without prejudice— that means nothing will be held against you should you try again another season. Of course, I hope you will feel about these workouts as I do—that they are worth the time and effort. And always keep in mind that some of you will develop so that you will help our varsity team sooner or later."

The coach's gaze roamed over the group. Slats wondered if he imagined that Long's eyes rested on him longer than on other boys.

"Moving the ball is one of the most important fundamentals of team play," Long went on. "There are primarily two ways of moving the ball—dribbling and passing. Passing is much the faster. It is more a team effort, and basketball is first a team game. So we start working on fundamentals with passing. Since the two-hand chest pass is basic for other passes, we drill on that type first."

The coach held the basketball between his hands, illustrated each point of technique. Fingers well spread to control the ball. . . . Kept as long as possible close to your body to make it harder for an opponent to knock it away. . . . Use hands, arms, shoulders, body and legs to give power to the pass. . . . Normally start the pass from chest-high, but not in all instances. . . . Depends on the maneuver involved, the build of the passer. . . . Can be started from as low as stomach or thighs.

"A quick snap makes the pass more effective," he said. "This snap comes mostly from the wrists. In order to impart spin and snap to make a good pass, keep the wrists loose.

"Form two lines facing each other. Start at one end and snap a two-hand pass across to the man opposite you in the other line. He snaps a pass back to the second man in the first line and so on. When the end of the line is reached, start passing the other way. All right, let's go!"

At first it was fun. There were inevitably bad passes, fumbles. Coach Long kept up a running comment, did not criticize, singled out a few passers for praise.

"Keep it going! . . . Hot potato, get rid of it! . . . When you fumble, go after it! . . . You have to keep your eye on the ball! . . . Way to go, Mike! . . . Grab that thing when you can reach it! . . . Good pass, good pass! . . . Watch it, Slats! You're tall enough to snag high passes!"

After a while any element of fun disappeared.

The ball became a round demon that taunted Slats. His arms and hands weighed twenty pounds each; the ball was made of lead. It struck his hands like it was shot from a cannon. Perspiration oozed from every pore, gathered in little rivulets and streamed down his face and body.

Slats thought they snapped two-hand chest passes for hours before Coach Long blew his whistle.

"All right," Long said. "Not too bad, for a first work-out. Some of you are really in there. Now, the other method of moving the ball is by dribbling. I'm sure all of you know that a dribble is the act of pushing the ball against the floor so that it rebounds and you control the bounce again and again.

"Good dribbling means a lot more than pushing the ball against the floor. In order to be a good dribbler, you must know how to pivot; how to change direction of your dribble; how to fake and change your pace. There is no such thing as instant perfection. It takes a lot of practice and more practice to acquire the talents a good dribbler must have."

The coach proceeded to illustrate techniques while he talked. Control of the ball is most important. . . . Start the dribble from a comfortable position. . . . You can't stand flat-footed or back on your heels. . . . The knees are bent slightly in order that the body may be swung in any direction. . . .

Ball well out in front. . . . Height of bounce con-trolled with cushions of fingers and hand. . . . Wrist loose and flexible. . . . The arm not directly used in the dribble does not just hang. . . . Hold it out for protec-tion, ready to snag the ball in case it is deflected by an opponent.

"Good dribbling is really an art," Coach Long said. "You just do not start bouncing a ball and become an instant dribbler. There are a lot of little things. But we can't learn until we start. Form the same lines you were in for the passing drill.

"Now, we will be at one end of the floor facing the opposite end. A boy from each line takes a ball, dribbles the length of the floor, shoots at the basket, grabs the rebound or the ball as it drops through the netting, and dribbles back to this end. Then he passes to the boy now at the head of his line."

Coach Long tossed a basketball to the first player in each line and another ball to the second boy in each line. His eyes sparkled.

"Give the first man time to dribble across the center line before you start," he told each second boy. "Everybody keep your eye on the ball you're dribbling. See which line finishes first. All right, start!"

Again it was fun at the beginning. Collisions occurred as boys chased erratic bounces. Dribbles went awry and dribblers banged into other dribblers. It was not as taxing as the pass drill. Then abruptly it was *more* taxing.

Where did all the basketballs come from? There had to be more than four. It was more like forty dribblers running up and down the floor. Slats was soon panting. Then his chest heaved; his hands became sweat-slippery. The ball seemed to be alive and trying its best to get away from him. The gold initials on his sleeveless jersey contrasted sharply to the sweat-darkened green when Coach Long finally whistled an end to the drill. Boy, who ever came up with a term like Neversweats for a gang that worked like this!

"Every workout of teams I coach closes with shooting free throws," the coach said. "You're all breathing harder than normally, more or less tense as you would be most times when you get a free throw in a game. Use all the baskets. I want each of you to take twenty-five free throws after every workout, before you go to the showers."

Slats was surprised when the coach tossed him a ball.

"Watch Salvatore," the coach told his Neversweats. "The underhand toss is probably the most accurate for free throwing. That doesn't mean everyone should adopt the underhand toss. If you are more comfortable shooting one-handed, or using a two-handed chest shot —use it.

"Whatever type shot you use, train yourself to relax when you toe the free throw line. Some players find that shaking their hands rapidly and taking a deep breath prior to shooting helps them to get loose. Try it. If it works for you, fine. All right, Salvatore, show us how it's done."

Slats dropped only five of his first ten tries through the hoop. He took more care and made eight of the second ten. Then the ball failed to find the netting three of his final five efforts.

"You have to concentrate to be at all consistent," Coach Long observed. "And practice, practice, practice."

Slats wondered if the coach was really regarding him with more interest than he usually showed Neversweats. Probably it was his imagination.

Slats showered, changed to street clothing and rode his bike to the Walker residence. Ron was outside when Slats wheeled the bicycle into the driveway. Ron handed Slats a piece of notebook paper.

"All the names are in the booklet," Ron said. "I copied EVERYTHING it has about each name, and I copied what your names mean and where they come from, too."

"I wish you'd look up Coach Long's, too. One of his names has to mean a slavedriver!"

"Well, maybe you could make something like that out of it. According to the book, Raymond means strong man. Quiet, peaceful and wise protector. Take the strong and protector together, you might say—"

"Yeah!" Slats' grunted exclamation interrupted Ron. "Protector—against any guy ever having a thought of taking things easy! I bet his last name comes from how long a guy can stand his quiet, peaceful slavedriving!"

He read the paper Ron had given him. Ludmilla —Slavonic origin. Means People's love. Nada—Slavonic. Hope. Enrico—Italian. Form of Henry. Home ruler.

That 'home ruler' thing was right, and Mom's names sure fit. At the bottom of the page were the derivation and meaning for his own names. Slats read aloud, "Durand—From Latin. Means lasting, enduring. Used to hardships. Stanislaus—Slavonic. Glory of the State. Salvatore—Latin. Saviour."

Suddenly Ron's face lit up with excitement. "That's it! You're the saviour of the basketball team for the glory of the state. And the state is our very own Lincoln Junior High!"

Slats couldn't believe his ears. "That's the craziest thing I've heard you say yet! You better stop writing so much and look at the facts. Why, that's about as accurate as Long's peaceful and quiet! But if I survive a couple more Neversweats' workouts, I'll believe that Durand means 'lasting and enduring'."

He put one foot on the bike pedal and prepared to shove off.

"Maybe some guys just get stuck with the wrong names!"

CHAPTER THREE

☐ *YOU WANT TO KNOW SOMETHING?*

Ron Walker greeted Slats Salvatore at the door. Ron noted that nothing was tucked beneath the tall boy's arm—such as a cardboard box used by bakeries to package pastries—and that his hands were empty of sack or other container.

"Been waiting for you," Ron said. He put on exaggerated expression of disappointment and sighed. "I was sure you'd bring a roll-cake or two."

"Yeah." Slats inclined his head. "I told Mom your invite to come over and watch the basketball game on television was only good if I brought roll-cakes."

He made a move as though to retreat instead of to enter the open doorway. "You didn't!" Ron gasped. He clutched Slats' arm. "Oh, migosh! If my mother gets an idea that I even thought of hinting at anything like that, she for sure will—"

Slats tried but he was just not able to keep his face straight. Ron broke off, gave his friend a penetrating look, then drew in a long breath and let it out. The panic faded from Ron's eyes; he pushed his glasses higher on his nose.

"You—you—," he sputtered. "Somehow a fellow doesn't expect a put-on from you. When am I going to wise up that you're a regular joker!"

"Mom told me to hurry along over here so I wouldn't miss the kickoff," Slats said. The grin on his longish face widened as he shook his head. "She meant tipoff, I guess. It's all the same to Mom. She wouldn't know a place-kicked football field goal from a basketball field goal sunk on a long shot—and she couldn't care less.

"She also told me to bring you over to our place after the game."

"And it happens she was mixing the filling for a batch of roll-cakes when I left. You can plan on eating a couple warm from the oven."

He grinned down at Ron, added, "Okay to come in now?"

"You over-size clown! Get in here before I break

your arm!" Ron pulled Slats through the doorway. "The television is tuned to the right channel and it's time for the pre-game show. According to the CITY NEWS T.V. page, it ought to be right down your alley. Hank Monzetti is going to be on the show. He's the Big Man that Western State started at center in their conference opener last week."

The television camera panned a full length view of Western State's skyscraper center. Then in order to get the interview in the picture, Monzetti was shown upward only from the green elastic web that held his gold basketball pants snug. The considerable expanse of gold jersey with green numerals and green piping around the neck and arm openings did nothing toward minimizing the height of Hank Monzetti.

"Why, Western State has the same colors that Lincoln Junior High has!"

"Yeah," Ron said, "Great stuff, a big university borrowing our colors, huh?" Then as he saw bewilderment come into Slats's eyes, Ron said contritely, "Sorry. I keep forgetting that you're new down here.

"Actually, it's the other way around. I was in Seventh Grade when the student body voted on what Lincoln Junior High would adopt as school colors. Coach Long came in wearing his Western State letter jacket. That beautiful gold jacket with green trimming and a big green WS monogram must have impressed other kids as much as me. Green and Gold got more than twice as many votes as all the other color combinations voted on."

The television screen showed the interviewer eying Monzetti from basketball shoes to straight black hair. He whistled, said, "Wow! You *are* a big one. Seven footers are getting more common-place, they tell me. But you are the first truly seven-footer-plus that I personally have encountered. You're not just tall, you're BIG!"

"I've always been big," Monzetti said. "And awkward. I've slaved and worked and slaved more to get so I don't stumble over my own feet—or foul the heck out of guys on the other teams!"

Lettering on the cover of a booklet showed as the television man read from it. Television, Radio and Press Brochure—Western State Basketball. "Hank Monzetti. Age 18. Freshman. 7 feet 1 inch tall. Weight 214." He glanced up at the young giant. Right statistics?"

Monzetti nodded.

"Western's Sports Information Director told me there is an interesting sidelight on your name," the interviewer continued. Will you tell us about it?"

For an instant the big basketball player looked embarrassed. Then he shrugged and went on. "My full name is Angelo Enrico Monzetti, Jr. Enrico is Italian for Henry; that's where the Hank comes from. My grandfather grew up in the same section of San Francisco as Hank Luisetti. Luisetti's given names were Angelo Enrico. Grandfather named my father after the area's most famous personality. So, in a sort of second-time-around way, I'm named after Hank Luisetti."

"The *great* Hank Luisetti." The television man nodded. "Every basketball buff knows what Hank Luisetti did for basketball. I am being signaled that our time is up. Thank you very much, and here is a wish that Angelo Enrico Monzetti, Jr. has some of the magic with a basketball that his fabulous namesake owned."

The TV screen changed to show a view of the crowd in Western State Field House, where the game being televised would take place. A commercial came after the crowd scene. Slats Salvatore said, "Who was Hank Luisetti?"

"I don't know," Ron admitted. "The guy said that every basketball buff knows what Luisetti did for basketball. They call anybody that's nuts about any sport a buff of that sport, so I must be a basketball buff. I'd better find out. Dad bought me a book last summer when we visited the Basketball Hall of Fame. It's bound to have stuff about Hank Luisetti. I'll get it when there's another timeout, or between halves."

Western State took an early lead in the televised game. Hank Monzetti tipped the opening tipoff to a teammate. Western set up a play pattern that got a man free in the corner. He missed the shot but Hank Monzetti barreled in and tapped the ball over the basket rim. No one could have said that Monzetti failed to make use of his height. He blocked shots. His tall bulk looming between them and the basket intimidated rival shooters into hurried efforts, and more often than not it was Monzetti who snagged the rebound.

Less than four minutes of play passed when Monzetti grabbed a rebound from the offensive board, flipped the ball to a teammate who counted a field goal and was fouled on the shot. He dropped the free throw through the cords; the three-point play gave Western State a ten-point lead and the other team called time out.

"Monzetti's slaving and working sure paid off," Ron Walker observed. "See what Coach Long means by possession of the ball being the name of the game? That big bozo is controlling both backboards. Western has possession of the ball most of the time. I'll get my book."

Slats had time only to note the title of the book before the timeout ended. BASKETBALL: THE GAME AND FAMOUS STARS.

Hank Monzetti continued to dominate play. Blocking shots or hurrying shooters into off-balance efforts, the giant freshman effectively blunted the opponent's offense. He grabbed rebounds off the backboards and gained possession of the ball for his team time after time.

At the end of the first half Western State enjoyed a lead of eleven points. Ron Walker thumbed through the book and found Hank Luisetti discussed in the first chapter of the section devoted to Famous Stars.

Angelo Enrico Luisetti: first real basketball hero. Luisetti's spectacularly accurate one-handed shot astounded the eastern seaboard—the supposed stronghold of basketball—and sparked a change of basketball from a stylized, somewhat stuffy game to the wide-open sport it has become today.

Before Luisetti brought a perfected one-handed shot to basketball, coaches everywhere

taught the two-handed shot exclusively. Nat Holman, a great performer with the Original Celtics, coached basketball at City College of New York. In 1936 word of the phenomenal one-handed shooting of Hank Luisetti filtered eastward from the Pacific Coast. Holman stated flatly that: "Nobody can tell me shooting with one hand is sound basketball. They will never get me to teach it to my boys."

Stanford University, with its star player Hank Luisetti, came east in 1936 to meet C.C.N.Y. in Madison Square Garden. Hank Luisetti made Holman "eat his words." The Stanford star counted 15 points in a 45–31 upset. The great bulk of Luisetti's point total came from his one-hand shot.

By today's standards of players marking up thirty-to-fifty points, Luisetti's total does not seem impressive. But in 1936 his total was more than many whole teams scored!

It was to be expected that after witnessing Luisetti's devastating one-handed shooting, coaches and players became believers. Six feet three and one-half inches, the San Francisco waterfront product really changed the game. . . .

There was a great deal more in the book about Luisetti. His records; offers he had to play professionally even years after he had graduated. But Slats Salvatore was thinking more about Hank Monzetti than Hank Luisetti as he and Ron watched the second half of the televised game.

. . . . always been big and awkward . . . .
slaved and worked and slaved more to get so I don't
stumble over my own feet—or foul the heck out of guys
on the other team. . .

I know another fellow who has always been big
and awkward, Slats thought. Maybe if he slaved and
worked and slaved more, Salvatore could get so he
didn't foul the heck out of guys on the other team.

"That's it." Ron Walker's observation came as the
televised game ended. "A 22-point Western win, which
was at least 90 percent Monzetti. You want to know
something?"

"Yeah." Slats nodded. "Mom's batch of roll-cakes
is out of the oven. So, we'd better get over to our place
right now."

Ron grinned, said, "Well, I'll buy that. But what I
was going to say was that you could be Lincoln Junior
High's Hank Monzetti. All you need is belief in Slats
Salvatore and get so you don't—"

"—foul the heck out of guys on the other teams."
Slats interrupted Ron. He eyed his blond friend, then
asked, "You want to know something? I'm going to
slave and work and slave and—what was it Coach Long
said you need for consistency? Concentrate, yeah that's
it. I'm going to slave and work and concentrate and just
maybe—well, who can say?"

CHAPTER FOUR

□ WORK AND SLAVE— AND BE CONNED!

SLATS BORROWED the book from Ron. After they each devoured two roll-cakes and Ron went home, Slats leafed through the book. There was much more in *Basketball: The Game and Famous Stars* than facts about Hank Luisetti and other famous players.

Chapters on Passing. Dribbling. Shooting. Rebounding—Slats remembered that rebounding was one thing Coach Long stressed. He settled down to read.

> Offensive rebounding is going after the ball when you or a teammate misses a shot at the opponents' basket. Recovery of the ball may provide another try for a basket. . . .
>
> Defensive rebounding is going after the ball when an opponent shoots at your basket and misses. Possession of the ball here is most important. Prevent a second shot for opponents, but most of all gain possession of the ball and get it out of danger right away!
>
> Every basketball player must be a rebounder. But you could be a natural passer, a natural dribbler, a natural shooter—and still not be a good rebounder. . . . Nature may have provided you

with valuable assets—height, leg muscles that enable you to jump high, good hands, aggressiveness. However, so many skills are involved in good rebounding that it is doubtful there should be such a designation as natural rebounder. Every player must develop his skill.

Here are a few tips that may help you develop effective rebounding.

FOR EFFECTIVE REBOUNDING

1. Positioning is fundamental. You could be ten feet tall and able to outjump a kangaroo and still be ineffective as a rebounder if you were rarely in proper position. Place yourself under the basket in the most advantageous spot to keep from being blocked out by an opponent.
2. Your jump must be timed, or it is wasted.
3. You should reach the ball at its highest point before starting down.
4. Once you have the ball it becomes MOST IMPORTANT. Cherish it. Protect it from rude grabs opponents will make. Be very sure that you have firm possession of that inflated sphere.
5. A basketball can and does take funny bounces. It will often happen that you cannot grab the ball securely when it comes off the board. The main effort must always be directed toward obtaining possession of it, but a secondary consideration of high priority is to tip the sphere away from the grasp of an opponent, if you cannot control it.

6. Once you have the ball firmly in your possession, don't "mess around." No fancy-Dan fakes; no spectacular behind-the-back-dribbling. Get the basketball away from under-the-basket traffic right now. One caution: don't be overanxious and earn an official's call for traveling.
7. Practice will smooth the rough edges. So, foremost is to practice, *practice* and PRACTICE!

About the same as Hank Monzetti's Work and Slave deal, Slats thought. There you are, Salvatore. All you need is to absorb it. Just follow Monzetti's work-and-slave and practice, *practice*, PRACTICE—and you'll have it made.

Any practice session under Coach Long was well organized, Varsity or Neversweats. He allowed a period of free basket shooting as a warmup before drills started. Basketballs thumped off the backboards at each end of the playing court and basketballs banged against practice backboards hung outside the playing area. But even during the free shooting the stocky coach circulated among the boys, seeming to see everything, spilling a constant stream of coaching tips.

"Get off the floor when you shoot a jumper, the follow through helps accuracy. . . . Try to be poised and ready to go after a rebound if your shot misses. . . . Up, up, use your height. . . . You can't wham the ball against the boards on a lay-up. Use your wrists, twist it up there feather-light. . . . Tip the ball, Salvatore, tip it! You aren't trying to knock the basket off the backboard! . . . Up! Up! Push the ball at the high point of your leap and make your jumper that much tougher to defense. . . ."

After a few minutes of basket shooting the Neversweats went through a brisk passing drill. Then the dribbling drill.

Finally Long brought a portable blackboard from under the bleachers. Four representations of the basket and free throw areas were painted permanently on the blackboard; circles numbered 1 to 5 were chalked in diagrams occupying each representation.

"I expect my teams to take advantage of opportunities for a fast break," the coach said. "There are two types of fast break, fire-engine and conservative. The fire-engine fast break sends all five men tearing downcourt when an opponent's rebound is taken off our board.

"This type of fast break is beautiful when control of the ball is maintained and a basket comes at the end. The big trouble is that the flashy attack too often breaks down. A hurried pass, a careless pass—and the other team gets the ball. With five men downcourt, your team is wide-open for the opponent's attack when possession of the ball is lost."

Long stopped speaking a moment while he looked around the group. Then he continued.

"We will follow the more conservative type of fast break. At least one—often two—men remain back in position for defense in case things clog up and our fast break opportunity is lost. It is my personal opinion that when three men breaking downcourt can't beat one or two defenders and get a lay-up shot, there was no real fast break opportunity. Slow break patterns to work a man into shooting territory must be developed. These diagrams are play patterns designed to do that."

The coach lifted a pointer from the chalk-holding groove at the bottom of the portable blackboard. He used the pointer to indicate on a diagram while he continued speaking.

"Center is numbered 1," he said. "Forwards are numbered 2 and 3, guards are numbered 4 and 5. The paths of players are shown by solid lines; broken lines indicate paths of passes. Study the diagrams, then we will walk through them. Xeroxed copies of these four patterns have been given to each boy on the varsity squad and each of you will receive a copy."

After the boys studied the diagrams chalked on the blackboard a while, Coach Long commented further.

"Any number of variations can be made from these basic patterns. You will note that 'depending on the reactions of the defense' appears at the end of each explanation. You will develop ability to change the pattern of attack according to the defense reactions. I hope you will never try to force a pass, or a shot, simply because a diagram calls for it at that point. Experience will teach you. So, we had better begin accumulating experience."

COACH LONG'S BASIC PLAY PATTERNS

Pattern #1—Number 5 passes to Number 1 and cuts into the free throw lane. He screens for Number 4 or takes a pass, depending on the reaction of the defense.

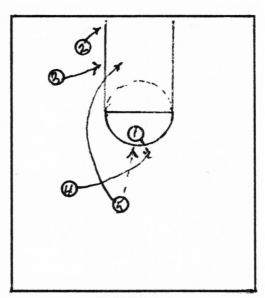

Pattern #1

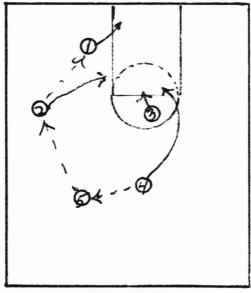

Pattern #2

41

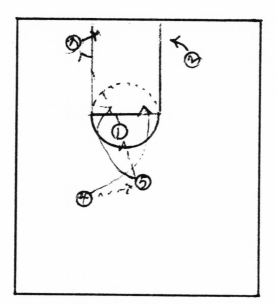

Pattern #3

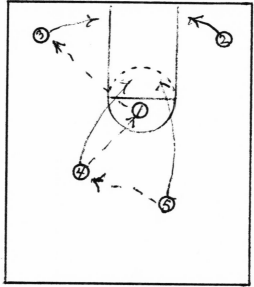

Pattern #4

Pattern #2—Number 4 passes to Number 5, cuts into the foul circle behind Number 3 for a possible return pass, acts as decoy or screen for Number 3. Number 5 passes to Number 2. Number 2 passes to Number 1 and cuts for the basket to screen or rebound, depending on the reaction of the defense.

Pattern #3—Number 4 passes to Number 5 and cuts into the foul circle to decoy or screen. Number 5 passes to Number 1 and cuts into the foul circle to decoy or screen. Number 1 passes to Number 3, or shoots, depending on the reaction of the defense.

Pattern #4—Number 5 passes to Number 4 and cuts into foul circle to decoy or screen. Number 4 passes to Number 1 and cuts into foul circle. Number 1 passes to Number 3, if he does not shoot, depending on the reaction of the defense.

Coach Long had the boys walk through the play patterns. Even walking, Slats Salvatore was confused. Long said, "You're the center, Salvatore, always Number 1."

"Yes, sir. But one time he is way down near the basket. I'm too stupid to know which time, I guess."

Coach Long looked at the tall boy for a moment, then pursed his lips and shook his head. "Overcoaching again," he said. "Why wouldn't you be confused? I neglected to tell you that some player will always signal which pattern is to be followed. We may use a hand signal or—there I go again!"

Raymond Long, only two years away from highly sophisticated collegiate basketball, shook his head a second time. "Maybe I will eventually learn that junior high players are not as slick or experienced as college men," he said. "Later, one boy—whoever shows the best leadership—will call out the number of the pattern. For this workout, I will call."

He divided the boys into three groups of five. Each of the teams took turns, went into action when the coach tossed the ball against a backboard and yelled which boy was to take the rebound. Then Coach Long shouted, "Number One," or whatever pattern he wanted them to follow.

Not once did the Neversweats work a pattern smoothly.

But at the close of the workout, the coach told them they had improved.

Anyone would need a microscope to see how much, Slats thought. Long is as good at conning as Ron Walker!

CHAPTER FIVE

□ TRIPLE THREAT

SLATS MUST have looked as low as he felt when Ron Walker came across the street to the Salvatores'. The smaller boy gave Slats a penetrating look, then pushed his glasses higher on his nose.

"You look something like a guy who's just been told his mother is never going to make any more roll-cakes," Ron said.

Slats shook his head and tried to grin. "Mom baked a batch this morning. Come on in and—"

"Hold it!" Ron threw back the shock of blond hair that tumbled over his forehead. "Blame it, I didn't come over to cadge a roll-cake. Get your chin off your shoe-tops, pal. What gives?"

"This basketball thing," Slats said morosely. "It's crazy!"

"Then there sure must be a lot of crazy guys. Pro basketball teams, college teams, YMCA teams, high school teams, junior high teams, teams of kids in church leagues and—"

"I meant crazy for me," Slats said. He looked accusingly at Ron. "That guff you fed me about the team needing height and how I need confidence and my name meaning saviour!" Slats threw up his hands in a gesture of disgust. "The other guys need a saviour from me!"

"*You're* crazy, not basketball, if you believe you aren't being helped by being out for the team. Okay, so something special is bugging you. Give. You'll feel better."

Slats told how he continually bumped into boys when he was trying to run patterns. "I make more miserable passes than decent ones, too. I fumble the ball all over the floor when I try to dribble. Everytime I go after a rebound I knock somebody down. Coach says practice smooths the rough spots—how does a fellow practice smoothing rough *spots* when he's been one gangly, clumsy *lump* all his life? My rough spots are getting *rougher!*"

"Look," Ron said, "you've been telling me how things Coach has the Neversweats do are explained pretty good in that book Dad bought me at the Hall of Fame, right?"

"So?"

"So, you come over to our place every night and practice. A long time ago Dad fastened a backboard and basket above our garage door, hoping I'd maybe be a basketball player. It's still there. We can turn on the driveway floodlight. I'm no good at shooting or dribbling or passing. But I can throw the ball back for free throws and toss it against the backboard and stuff like that. You can concentrate like Coach told you on free throwing and smoothing the rough spots."

Slats considered briefly. He wanted desperately to 'smooth the rough spots.' After a moment or two, he said, "It's a deal, on one condition. When you get fed up with being knocked around, you say so."

They practiced passing. Slats dribbled up the driveway and tried boring in for lay-up shots. He blew nine of twelve tries. While he was breathing hard from the dribbling, Slats stepped to the mark still faintly visible on the concrete to represent a free throw line. He shook his hands vigorously and took a deep breath before each try.

He dropped ten straight through the hoop.

"You sure don't have to smooth any rough spots for free throwing," Ron said.

"I've been concentrating. It's the one thing I'm any good at. It's other stuff I fall flat on my face trying— like rebounding without fouling!"

"Okay, so concentrate on rebounding. It works for free throwing, it'll work for other stuff."

Ron tossed the ball against the backboard and Slats roared in for rebounds. He came down clutching the ball five of six efforts and would have probably got the other except the sphere hit exactly in the space between the metal ring and the backboard and stayed there.

It was no problem for Slats to leap and tip the ball from its balanced position. Ron said, "Great going. I can't see the big beef about not doing the rebounding thing."

"Well, it's easy to grab the ball when there is no opposition to foul, and stuff."

Ron eyed his tall friend, shrugged and said, "It's all in a good cause, so I'll go after the rebounds, too."

The very first effort was disastrous.

Ron jumped as high as he could. Unfortunately his leap carried him into the path of Slats' drive. Ron bounced off Slats like a pingpong ball off the top of the net—flat. Seeing Ron crash to the concrete drive made Slats forget the basketball. He was standing over his friend's sprawled figure instantly.

"You all right?" Slats asked anxiously.

Ron groaned, sat up and felt tenderly at one shoulder. He attempted a grin but it did not quite come off.

He said, "I'll live. But I think I'd better say 'so' while I'm still all in one piece!"

For an instant Slats looked puzzled. Then he remembered. "So it is. Let's quit for today." He grinned ruefully. "Guess I'm going to be a triple threat star."

Ron frowned. "That's as cockeyed as your mother sending you over in time for the kickoff of a basketball game! Mixing sports must run in your family. Triple threat is a football term. It means a back who is a threat to run, kick or pass when the center snaps the ball to him."

"I know." Slats nodded. "Dad played football in high school. He told me he was a triple threat back, the kind a famous All American back at Notre Dame said *he* was when he was disgusted with himself—a threat to trip, stumble or fumble."

Slats sighed, added glumly, "Well, I'm that kind of threat in basketball—to bumble, jumble or foul!"

CHAPTER SIX

☐ ON THE VARSITY SQUAD

THE CLASS Slats went to before Physical Education met in the room farthest from the gymnasium. Mr. Raymond Long, Boys' Physical Education teacher, was as tough on late arrivals for his classes as Coach Raymond Long was at basketball workouts. It was a daily challenge for

Slats to get into gym gear and upstairs before the "tardy whistle" sounded.

Ron Walker's and Slats' lockers were side by side. Ron was tieing the laces of his gym shoes when Slats raced in and slammed his locker door open. Ron looked up and asked eagerly, "Is there a new notice on the bulletin board?"

"I don't know. I never have time to look at the thing."

Slats began changing hurriedly to green gym pants and shirt.

"There wasn't anything new when I looked," Ron said. "But there will be any time now."

Slats said nothing.

"How you doing on the Neversweats free throw chart?" Ron asked.

Slats looked at the smaller boy and frowned. "What's all this business about notices on the bulletin board and where I am on the free throw chart?" he asked. "Not that it matters, but I finally made the top with 20 out of 25 yesterday. Incidentally, the chart is for varsity and Neversweats combined."

"That I didn't know," Ron admitted. "That's great. Probably they know over at the Kid Sports Page desk at CITY NEWS. I'll—"

A rasping sound came from the instrument below the locker room clock. Ron broke off and rushed with Slats to the stairway leading to the gymnasium. Roll-call for ninth grade Physical Education class came two minutes after the warning buzzer sounded.

"I think I know something you don't," Ron said

as they hurried up the stairs, "but you should find out from—well, not from me. If Mr. Long meets this class, then I've been yakking from 'way out in left field. But if there is a substitute teacher, then for sure there will be a new notice on the bulletin board."

The teacher in charge of ninth grade Physical Education that day was a woman entirely unknown to Slats. She called the roll, then explained to the class.

"Mr. Long is attending a meeting. It was decided at the last moment that I would take his sixth hour class so he could leave early."

"Mr. Long left a multiple choice test on material he has covered the past eight weeks of physiology and personal hygiene.

"When you complete your papers, you are free to leave. I'm sorry there was no time to notify you that changing clothing was not necessary."

Slats and Ron finished their tests almost at the same time. Back in the locker room, before they could begin stripping for a shower, Ron clutched Slats' arm and steered him to the door. The bulletin board had been cleared of everything but one notice. Slats read the brief message.

BASKETBALL MEN
There will be no varsity or Neversweats
workouts today. All varsity squad members
report tomorrow (Saturday) 10 A.M. at the
gymnasium. Durand Salvatore and Michael
Kazerski of the Neversweats squad also report.
Raymond Long

Slats read the notice quickly, started to turn away, then did a double-take. *Durand Salvatore and Michael Kazerski of the Neversweats also report.* He had not just imagined that he saw his name. It was on the notice—DURAND SALVATORE!

Ron was grinning. "I knew it!" He said, "Congratulations. Look's like you're on your way."

"Man, ain't that something else!" The boys turned at the words from a boy standing behind them. "I was sure hoping I'd make it this year," Mike Kazerski said.

Mike was solidly built, a full head shorter than Slats but probably heavier. His hair was too dark to be called blond, too light to be called brown. Steady gray eyes were set in a broad, square-cut face.

"I have to give you the credit, Salvatore," Kazerski said. "I sweat blood with the Neversweats all last year and it looked as though I'd bleed dry this year and still be with the Neversweats. Then you came along with that underhand free throw and I stole your stuff. I practiced aiming at the center of the basket instead of the backboard. I figure it was when I climbed on the free throw chart to be second only to you that Coach noticed—"

"Wait a second!" Ron Walker interrupted. He looked at Slats then back at Mike Kazerski. "I've been thinking I knew something you guys didn't. You talking about Coach moving you to the varsity as maybe backup man to Slats, Kazerski?"

"Coach sent me to the Neversweats because I couldn't shoot for beans." Mike Kazerski's face mirrored bewilderment. "I was going to say he noticed I'm hitting free throws AND from the floor. I don't know from nothing about what you just said."

"What the heck is this backup stuff?" Slats asked.

Ron drew in a breath and let it out. "Okay, here is the scoop," he said. "The editor of the Kids Sports Page got an idea—the CITY NEWS would promote an annual free throw competition. Every junior high in the City League and every junior high in the County League would pick a guy to represent them. A backboard and basket would be set up on the stage of Municipal Auditorium so nobody could beef about a home court advantage. The thing has been up in the air for weeks.

"This noon when I turned in a piece, the editor gave me a note to bring to school for Coach. He said he hadn't been able to reach Coach by phone and it was imperative that he get the message before he left for the meeting."

Ron hesitated, seemed to be reassuring himself when he went on.

"He knew I saw what he wrote to Coach and didn't say anything about it being a secret, or anything. The message was that the free throw competition had been okayed by the editor-in-chief. A CITY NEWS photographer will be at the gym tomorrow morning to take a team picture. He will also get shots of guys most likely to represent Lincoln."

Kazerski said, "Now, I get it. Maybe Coach *did* move me up so I would be Slats' backup. The coach would want Lincoln's representative to be from the varsity squad, not from the Neversweats. So he moved both of us up because we're the top free throwers."

A little space of time went by. Slats was staring at the notice. *Durand Salvatore . . . . also report.* He could hardly believe he read the notice correctly. It was Mike Kazerski who broke the silence.

"Man, man!" He belted Slats' shoulder. "Am I ever glad you came along! I honestly hope it's you that represents Lincoln—and beats the pants off every other guy in the competition!"

CHAPTER SEVEN

☐ *PLAY IT COOL!*

SLATS SALVATORE and Ron Walker kneeled on the living room floor. Spread before them was the Kid Sports Page from the *CITY NEWS SPECIAL.*

JUNIOR HIGH BASKETBALL ROUNDUP stretched across the top of the page in headline-size black letters. *City Schools* was the subhead above a column of five group pictures of boys in basketball uniforms; *County Schools* headed a column of five similar pictures on the right side.

"It's the best Kid Sports Page ever," Ron said.

"Uh-huh," Slats mumbled. "Sure is hard to believe."

Ron frowned. The observation seemed a little on the strange side. He looked intently at Slats. A glassy expression held Slats' eyes, which were fastened on one of the smaller pictures. *Contenders For City-County Free Throw Title* was the heading.

Ron continued to watch Slats. "How now, brown cow. Now is the time for all good men to come to the aid of their country, wouldn't you say?"

"Yeah." Slats nodded. He did not raise his eyes from the small picture. *Salvatore, Lincoln* was printed below the picture. "It's really something. It's beautiful!"

Ron's laugh explosion penetrated Slats' haze. He looked up uncertainly.

Ron said, "Man, how high on Cloud Nine can you get! You have no idea what I asked, have you?"

Slats shook his head.

"I repeated a couple of lines our typing teacher had us doing over and over last week," Ron said. "Quote from you: It's really something. It's beautiful! Unquote."

Slats looked startled. He grinned, then sobered. "I didn't mean my picture is beautiful like you'd say a flower is beautiful, or something," he said. "I meant that—that—well, you know what I meant!"

"Sure." Ron nodded. "Making the varsity squad and getting your picture in the Special has to be beautiful. But you can't live up there on Cloud Nine, you know. You have to remember what it says here."

Ron indicated a paragraph below the pictures of *Contenders For City-County Free Throw Title*. Then he read aloud.

"Above are pictures of the boys most likely to represent their schools in the *City News* free throw competition. No set rule is imposed as to how competitors will be selected. Each coach will name the boy to represent his school.

"Washington Junior High's representative was named by their coach at the time the pictures were taken. Coach Long of Lincoln Junior High stated that the boy with the best score on the daily free throw chart they keep will represent the school—and that as of now one boy has a lead that he will probably maintain."

Ron stopped reading and regarded Slats. "You're *going* to keep that lead," Ron said. "Concentration, Coach said, didn't he? Okay. What you do is concentrate on tossing that round ball through the hoop until it's automatic—and we begin right now!"

They went to the Walker driveway. Slats sunk twelve tries before missing. He said, "That's better than I've done in practice."

Then he dropped twelve more through the ring.

"Twenty-four out of twenty-five." Ron nodded. " 'nuf said. You hit like that in the competition, you're a cinch to go all the way."

Slats said as though talking more to himself, "That concentration business works."

Ron said, "But you have to keep practicing. Let me take that book you borrowed."

"Sure, it's your book. But why?"

"I remember there is stuff in there about free throwing. I'm going to make a list so I can help by checking you out. You're going to win this free throw competition,—man!"

A voice interrupted. "I sure hope so—since this competition deal got him on the varsity." Butch Arnold was standing at the end of the driveway. "But remember, he's got to do a lot more than free throw to stay on!"

Varsity practice is not much different from Neversweats practice, Slats told himself—there's no sense in being nervous. Coach Long was prowling about the gymnasium, watching shots, giving coaching tips. It seemed that he never missed seeing a poor effort, or an essentially good one at any basket. The man had to have eyes in the back of his head!

"All right." The coach blew his whistle to end the free shooting. "As I'm sure you all know, play in the City League starts next week. We open at Washington. I believe it is a fair judgment that Washington is favored to win the City Championship and probably go on to take the City-County playoffs.

"They play zone defense. One way to beat a zone is to shoot over the defense. Successful outside shooting will force the defense to leave their stay-in-your-zone-and-wait-for-the-offense and come out after the ball. The zone is no good when you are behind on the scoreboard.

"Another way to beat the zone is to get men into areas of high percentage shooting before the defense can get back and form. Of course, that is another way of saying fast break."

What the heck, Slats thought. He as much as told

us we were not going to fast break the day he gave out the play patterns. What gives?

"The day I gave you play pattern diagrams I mentioned that we would never send all five men downcourt in a fast break." Long seemed to be answering the question Slats asked himself. "Such a fire-horse fast break is often disastrous. Hurried passing is likely to be poor passing. Loss of the ball on an attempted fire-horse break is a high risk and when it fails the other team usually gets an unguarded try at your basket.

"However, I also mentioned that a conservative fast break is essential to a well-rounded attack. When opportunities to fast break come in a game, we want to make use of them."

The coach discussed situations offering fast break opportunities.

"My college coach was a student of history," Long finished. "He was always bringing in some historical fact to illustrate some point about aggressive basketball. He compared the fast break with the principle followed by Mason Forest, a very successful Confederate leader in the War Between the States. Forest explained his successes in beating Union forces by saying, 'I get thar fustest with the mostest.'

"It doesn't just happen that you're there 'fustest with the mostest' in fast breaking. You plan and drill and drill and drill. We are going to drill every practice period. Here's how we will develop our fast break."

Coach Long named five boys to be the Shirts team. Slats Salvatore was one of the five the coach told to remove their shirts.

"Skins' ball out of bounds at the center line," Long said. "Try to work the ball in for a good shot. Make the basket and you retain possession of the ball. If the shot is missed, Arnold and Kraft go for the rebound. The passout is to Olson; Thrall and Jenkins break down the floor, one guard drags.

"A good outlet pass is the key to the fast break. Here we go!"

The Shirts forced a shot from the foul circle. It missed. Slats mistimed his leap and Butch Arnold grabbed the rebound. He whirled and powered a pass 'way beyond Olson's reach. The ball bounded across the floor and out of bounds. Long shrilled his whistle.

"Nice rebounding," he said. "But that pass!"

"You said the guy who gets the rebound passes out right away!" Arnold complained.

"*Passes* out, not just heaves the ball! You must know where you're passing. Okay. Shirts out of bounds. Work it in for a good shot."

Mike Kazerski worked free at the free throw circle and took a jumper. The ball hit the basket rim. Slats and Butch Arnold went after the rebound. A sharp elbow jab from Butch failed to keep Slats from coming down with the ball. He tried frantically to locate somebody without a shirt to pass the ball—and Butch Arnold tied him up. The whistle sounded.

"It is sure to cost any chance for a fast break if the outlet pass is delayed," the coach said. "You can't stand around. Try it again."

Try-it-again got so it rang in Slats' brain. Ragged, ragged play went on and on. It seemed to Slats that

Butch Arnold had at least a dozen elbows. Slats and Butch and Al Kraft went up after a rebound. Kraft crashed to the floor as Slats clutched the ball. Mike Kazerski raced downcourt and Slats fired a pass that led the former Neversweats mate just right. Spat, spat! Kazerski passed to a teammate, and he shot the ball to a third shirtless boy. The lone defensive man had to commit himself. He went after the boy with the ball who was dribbling toward the basket. A snappy pass back to Kazerski cutting around resulted in Mike Kazerski driving in for a lay-up basket.

"Good passing. Fine dribbling and faking," Coach Long said. "Salvatore, a charging foul would have probably been called against you in a game. It's a rough climate around the backboards, but every man is entitled to his spot. I did not see the contact, I only saw Kraft go down. However, there are two officials in a game and one of them would have caught the foul. Watch it. Shirts' ball. Try it again."

Coach Long kept them working on the fast break. He followed the play every second, coaxed them, pointed out mistakes, praised good passes or dribbles or fakes.

"Use your height . . . . get off the floor . . . . don't just heave the ball wildly . . . . please, please please keep your eyes open out there . . . . move! move! get the ball out! . . ."

The rugged physical struggle between Butch Arnold and Slats Salvatore went on. Finally the coach called a halt to the drill.

"We'll scrimmage," he said. "Two eight minute quarters, regular game procedure. Either team sees an opportunity, fast break."

Slats was called three times for charging, another time for holding. Once he beat Arnold cleanly and grabbed a rebound. He passed out quickly to a teammate near the center line. Al Kraft was caught alone before Olson could get back to help. Mike Kazerski took a sharp pass, faked Kraft neatly and drove in to lay the ball gently against the backboard. Good basket.

The final play before Coach Long whistled an end to the practice drowned any brief elation that Slats might have felt.

He disregarded Arnold's elbow jab and beat him for the rebound—then threw the ball six feet over a teammate's head and out of bounds.

That night before the free throw practice started in the Walker drive, Slats was so quiet that Ron finally said, "Now what the heck's bugging you?"

Slats said gloomily, "I guess things would be better all around if I just forgot about basketball, including the *CITY NEWS* competition."

"You have a bad time with chart free throwing today?"

Slats shook his head. "We didn't have the usual twenty-five, but I dropped ten straight while we were warming up. I just wonder whether I should be on the varsity. Arnold was right—there's more to it than free throwing."

Ron eyed his tall friend, shook his head then pushed at his glasses. "One time at varsity practice and everything would be better if you quit! Man, you're something else when it comes to bad-mouthing your-self. Makes no sense. What happened?"

"I'm just hopeless, that's the plain fact. I'll always be a gawky, awkward nothing!"

Before he really intended to, Slats poured out his anguish. "I happened to look at Coach right after that last horrible pass," he finished. "He was looking down at the floor, shaking his head."

"I suppose all the other guys took hold of the fast break thing like they'd been doing it forever?"

"Well, no. That is, Arnold and Kraft made some good passes and Mike Kazerski drove in for two swell lay-ups and sometimes things worked okay. But—" Slats' words trailed off.

Ron snorted. "But things didn't work all the time for everybody but you, huh? Nobody looked smooth and slick all the way. Why do you think Coach kept at the drill? You ever consider that he maybe shook his head because he was kinda disgusted with the whole gang not going so hot?"

Slats said nothing.

"Get with it, pal," Ron went on. "I sat in on the last part of the scrimmage. Butch Arnold worked you over pretty good, but you were getting in some good licks. The thing is, Arnold has had more experience and is more clever at dishing out contact and getting away with it. You still bugged over Arnold?"

"Well, he's so much better than I'll ever be! He's better for the team than—"

"Hold it!" Ron scowled, tossed his head to throw back the shock of blond hair that had fallen over his forehead. "Get out of your head that stuff about Arnold being so much better than Salvatore! Butch is good and wants to win—plays to win, all right. He was the big noise for Lincoln last year because he was the biggest man. Fact is, it'll be better for the team when you're both in there. What you gotta do is believe in Salvatore, hang in there—and play it cool, man!"

CHAPTER EIGHT

☐ FIRST GAME

SLATS SALVATORE sat on the end of the long bench in the visitors' dressing room at Washington Junior High gym. He glanced down at the shiny green basketball pants with gold piping down the sides and gold elastic around the top. His hand smoothed the green Number 12 on the front of a bright gold basketball jersey.

I'm really here in a Lincoln basketball outfit, he thought. Gosh, I might get into the game!

Other boys of the Lincoln varsity squad came and sat on the bench. Coach Long faced them. When he spoke Long's tone was calm and low.

"No pre-game fight talk," he said. "Any shortcomings that may show up could not be erased or even eased by a plea to go-out-and-give-your-all-for-dear-old-Lincoln. I hope we are reasonably well prepared from practice.

"We are starting the lineup we have worked mostly as Shirts in practice scrimmages. Thrall and Jenkins at forwards; Arnold, center; Kraft and Olson, guards. Substitutions will be made as I deem necessary."

The coach's eyes traveled from end to end of the bench for a short space of time.

"Washington has four of their regulars from last year playing today," he said. "They are a more experienced team, but I firmly believe we can play with them. Stay cool. Keep your poise. Don't be stampeded into making errors that will turn possession of the ball over to them. Olson is captain today. If and when he is out of the game, Kraft will act as captain."

Long held his left hand with fingers pointing horizontally, his right hand with fingers extended vertically touching the left palm.

"Just to be sure you fellows know the sign for time-out, this is it," he said. "I want the captain to look toward our bench once in a while, especially if the other team sinks two or three baskets in a row. When you see me making the sign, tell the nearest official we want time out.

"All right. We'll be shooting at the basket at the bleacher end of the court, the one we shot at during warmup. Just the five starters. When the referee blows his whistle to signify the game is about to begin, you starters come to the bench."

Olson led the squad through the door to the playing floor. As the boys emerged around the end bleachers, a blast of noise greeted them. Six cheerleaders leaped and clapped hands and exhorted Lincoln supporters in the stands.

Yea-a-a, Lincoln!
Yea-a-a, Lincoln!
Yea-a-a, Lincoln!
Yea, team! FIGHT!

Olson dribbled toward the basket, leaped and pushed a jumper from twenty feet out. The ball dropped through the netted metal ring. Lincoln fans exploded. Slats Salvatore tried to watch Thrall snake in the ball and put a layup against the backboard and the leaping cheerleaders at the same time. He half-stumbled over his own foot. Mike Kazerski steadied him.

Mike grinned, said, "They gave us a good old yea-a-a yell, anyway. You'll really go down when you hear some of the kooky ones!"

Each of the five Lincoln starters made their shot and each basket brought a staccato yea-a-a! from the stands. Then Washington players came out on the floor. And a louder roar filled the gym. Washington cheerleaders led a chant that was accompanied by stomping feet.

Beat 'em! Bust 'em! (stomp, stomp, stomp)
That's our custom! (stomp, stomp, stomp)
Washington! Washington! Washington!
RAH!

The referee consulted with the timer at the official's table. He blew a short blast of his whistle, bounced a new basketball while he walked to the center circle. Starting players of both teams trotted to their respective benches. Slats Salvatore was a little slow in joining the Lincoln reserves crowding around the starters. The ritual of players clasping hands over the coach's, the thumping of shoulders and pepper talk was entirely new to Slats.

"The old pepper, gang! . . . Everybody in there with the old fight! . . . Get the tip, Butch. We'll hit 'em with a quick bucket! . . . Let's go with the old jinegar! . . ."

The referee's whistle shrilled again. Players took position for the opening tipoff.

Butch Arnold stretched a teeny higher than the Washington center. He tipped the ball straight ahead. Pete Thrall cut across fast, slapped the ball ahead to his right into the hands of Bob Jenkins. Jenkins head-faked his guard and was around him.

Jenkins dribbled twice, leaped and laid the ball feather-light against the backboard above the metal hoop. The sphere dropped through the basket netting.

"Yea-a-a! . . . Way to go, Bob-boy! . . . Get some more! . . . Pour it to 'em! . . ."

Jubilant yells from boys on the Lincoln bench choked off even as they jumped to their feet. A Washington boy took the ball out of bounds beneath the basket. It seemed one continuous motion when he whipped a long pass downcourt. The pass was taken two strides behind Al Kraft. The Washington player dribbled on in and dumped an easy basket over the netted ring. A 2 showed on the scoreboard under Washington to match the 2 under Lincoln.

Washington players hurried into a 2–2–1 zone defense before Lincoln could fast break. They passed the ball around. Olson signaled play pattern Number Three. The defense forced a twenty foot shot by Thrall which missed. Butch Arnold was neatly boxed away from the rebound. It was grabbed by the Washington center.

The outlet pass was aimed at a forward; Olson intercepted. He was almost tied up, passed back to Jenkins. The tough zone defense again contained Lincoln's attack. Butch Arnold tried to drive past the Washington center, the back man in the 2–2–1 setup. Arnold was called for charging.

No free throw. Washington threw inbounds to their star center. A bounce-pass around Arnold to a teammate, dribble, sharp pass back to the center; a Washington basket.

Coach Long stood in front of the bench, making the timeout sign. Lincoln players gathered around him.

"They're positioning men to screen Arnold from rebounding," the coach said. "If they continue to get most of the rebounds, they could run us right out of the gym!"

Long flicked a glance toward Slats, seemed about to say something to him, then looked away. "We've got to get our share off the backboards," he finished. "Try to position yourselves so you are not blocked out."

After the timeout, Lincoln lost the ball on an intercepted pass. The Washington shot missed. Butch Arnold got his first rebound. His outlet pass was fast and sharp to Olson. The Lincoln fast break caught Washington's defense not in position. Thrall and Jenkins were "thar fustest with the mostest." A guard was forced to go after Thrall. His pass around the defender to Jenkins was perfectly timed. Jenkins cashed a layup basket.

Washington, 4; Lincoln, 4. The scoreboard clock showed barely 59 seconds played. That first minute apparently set a pattern for the game. The score was tied at 8–all, 11–11 and 13–all. Both teams played tough defense. At the end of the first quarter it was Washington, 14; Lincoln, 13.

No scoring at all at the beginning of the second period. Midway through the period, a Washington boy made the second of two free throws awarded when he was fouled in the act of shooting. Kraft threw the ball in bounds to Olson; Olson foolishly tried to pass cross-court. Washington intercepted and the easy layup basket gave them a 17–13 lead. Coach Long signaled for time out.

"You've been told a hundred times that cross-passing in front of our basket is dangerous," Long said when the boys gathered. "We cannot afford unnecessary turnovers!"

Two minutes of play passed with neither team scoring, but it was Washington's poor luck more than Lincoln's defensive skill. Jenkins was fouled while shooting. He made the first free throw, missed the second. Somebody batted the rebound deep; Al Kraft scooped up the loose ball, raced past a lunging Washington boy and loosed a jump shot from the free throw circle. The jumper was good, and he was fouled from behind. Kraft dropped the free throw through the netting. The three-point play tied the score again at 17–all.

Then Lady Luck turned her smile on Washington.

Olson committed a loose-ball foul. Lincoln's defense formed too quickly to allow a fast break. But Washington showed that they also had set play patterns.

They zipped short snappy passes. Butch Arnold was faked out of position. Slats Salvatore leaped from the bench and yelled, "Watch it! Jam up the middle! Jam up the middle!"

The Washington center took a fine pass at the foul circle and dribbled straight in. He eased a layup shot into the metal ring. Olson grabbed the ball, stepped out of bounds and heaved a wild pass. Washington intercepted. The Washington boy dribbled fast toward the Lincoln goal. Jenkins slanted across to close a wide path down the middle.

"Shoot! Shoot!" Players leaped up and down in front of the Washington bench and yelled. "Time's almost up!"

The boy with the ball stopped, aimed hurriedly and let fly a long shot. The ball arched toward the distant basket while the timer's horn sounded to end the quarter. It banged off the backboard, slanted against the front of the basket and fell through.

Washington, 21; Lincoln, 17.

The five boys starting the second half surrounded Coach Long. Slats Salvatore gripped somebody's hand. He was in a kind of unbelieving daze. The coach's words during halftime intermission echoed in his thoughts.

Nothing wrong with us that a few baskets won't cure. . . . We are still coming up short in rebounding. . . . Try to position yourselves so they can't screen you out. . . . We have to stop giving them room for easy drive-in layups. . . .

But mostly Slats was recalling what Coach said to him as they came from the dressing room.

"Report to the scorer, in for Olson. Jump center for the tipoff, then after that Arnold plays center. You yelled to jam the middle and I want you to do just that. Use your height to go after rebounds, of course. But your main job is to tear back and seal off the path through the foul lane. Don't let them fake you out of there. Cut off their drives through the lane."

The referee blew his whistle. Slats went to the center circle for the tipoff, and got his first taste of needling from rival players.

"Well, well, well! Fancy me having the honor of jumping against the Kid Sports Page Wonder!" The Washington center grinned broadly, then made a little shake of his head. "Man, are you ever going to wish this was free-throwing just for the chart with no opposition!"

Slats eyed the Washington star. Something had nagged him all through the first half about the guy. He's about the same height as Butch Arnold—I'm taller, Slats thought. I should be able to get higher than— Slats' eyes widened suddenly as he realized what had been nagging at the back of his mind. This guy's picture had also been on the Kid Sports Page Special.

"How about that?" Slats inclined his head. "You're the hot shot your coach picked without having to beat anybody!" Slats stuck out his hand. His grin was as wide as the other boy's. "Don't suppose it might turn out we'd both wish it was a free throwing deal with no opposition, do you?"

Apparently the Washington star had not expected a return along the same bantering line. He looked somewhat startled; his grin became slightly uncertain. He gripped Slats' hand briefly.

"Who you trying to put on?" he asked. "You would'a been in here from the start if you were all that good!"

Slats out-reached his rival on the tipoff. He pushed the ball ahead to Bob Jenkins. Jenkins dribbled twice and drilled a pass to Butch Arnold. Short pass to Thrall. Bounce pass around a defensive man back to Arnold. Swish!

Arnold's jumper dropped through the netting. Washington, 21; Lincoln, 19.

Slats had taken three strides upcourt when Jenkins grabbed the tipoff, in case there should be a rebound. He back-tracked quickly as Arnold's shot dropped in. Al Kraft was around the free throw circle. Washington did not attempt a fast break.

A guard dribbled across the center line. Short, snappy passes. Men weaving in and out trying to break into good shooting position. The Washington center took a pass at the head of the free throw lane. He made a head and shoulder fake to the right.

Long arms extended wide, Slats was still in the middle of the lane when the Washington star drove for the basket. He would have had to foul Slats to finish his drive. He stopped short, pivoted and looped a hook shot from just short of the fifteen foot line. The ball dropped through the netting without touching backboard or metal ring.

"That's how it's done, Salvatore!" The Washington boy crowed. "With or without opposition!"

Slats knew hook shots from that far out were not going to drop consistently. He also knew there would have been a clear path for a driving layup except for his slowness in reacting to the very good fake. This guy was good.

Lincoln's pattern attack blunted against the tough zone defense. Jenkins finally shot long over a guard, and hit. The teams jockeyed for position. The Washington center took a high pass at the top of the key. Again Slats forced a hook shot from well out.

The ball bounced off the rim of the basket. The shooter followed his shot in. Slats went up for the rebound. They banged solidly together but there was no whistle. Slats came down with the ball. He saw Arnold momentarily in the clear and sizzled the sphere to him.

It was a perfect outlet pass. Arnold flipped the ball to Thrall. Jenkins and Thrall bore down on the one guard who was back. He could not cope with the two-on-one setup. Jenkins cashed the fast break shot. Tie score, 23–all.

The lead see-sawed back and forth. Slats fouled a

forward in the act of shooting. He made both free throws. Jenkins sunk a Long Tom. Less than twenty seconds later he intercepted a poor pass and drove all the way in for an unguarded layup which gave Lincoln a 27–25 lead.

Slats tangled an arm around the Washington center's shoulder when he was trying for a tip-in. It was a two-shot foul and both free tosses dropped through the cords. The scoreboard showed Washington, 27; Lincoln, 27 when the third period ended.

Coach Long nodded satisfaction with his team's play when they came to the sideline between quarters.

"You're playing good basketball," he told them. "We're getting our share of rebounds. We aren't giving them the high percentage shots."

When the referee blew his whistle for the start of the final quarter, Long spoke to Slats. "You're doing a great job. Just don't foul out!"

Slats tried. But barely a minute of play passed before he was too aggressive in going after a rebound. Three personal fouls.

Washington's pass inbounds was wild. Thrall scooped up a loose ball, saw Jenkins cutting past his guard, zipped a well-timed pass to his teammate. Jenkins jumped and eased the ball over the basket rim. 29–27, Lincoln.

Hurried passes. Traveling calls against boys who were over-anxious. Wild shots. Neither team was able to score. The clock registered less than two minutes of playing time left when Arnold pivoted away from a Washington boy in midcourt. Whistles blew. His pivot had carried Arnold's foot across the center line into Lincoln's backcourt.

"Over and back." The referee made a motion to indicate the violation. "Washington ball out of bounds at the line."

They threw the ball in to their center. Slats ran beside him, tried to get ahead. The Washington star was faster. It may be that a more experienced player would have accepted the fact he was outmaneuvered. Slats instinctively threw out a long arm. He hooked the dribbler.

Both officials shrilled whistles. They raised fisted arms high to signal the foul. Fourth personal charged against Salvatore. Slats was out of the game. Then came the really bad part.

Lincoln had used up their allotment of team fouls. Washington would be awarded free throws from then on under the one-and-one rule. If the shooter made the first try, he would have a bonus shot.

The boy who would represent Washington in the *CITY NEWS* free throw competition stepped to the line. Calmly, as though it was a foregone conclusion, he dropped two free throws into the basket.

Tie score, 29–29.

Lincoln was ruined.

Washington's defense forced a long try that was way off. They brought the ball across the line, passed until the big center worked free in the lane. He drove in, made the layup basket and the score was 31–29 for Washington.

They wisely sat upon their lead.

Lincoln fouled attempting to get the ball. Washington hit a one-and-one. 33–29. Lincoln fouled again. Washington cashed another one-and-one.

Final score: Washington, 35; Lincoln, 29.

CHAPTER NINE

□ *ADVICE FROM RON*

RON'S EYES held a startled question when he jerked his gaze to Slats. "You aren't putting me on?" Ron asked. "You're really serious?"

"I don't see why you'd think I'm kidding."

"And I don't see why anybody *wouldn't* think you were." Ron shook his head. "Quote: I lost the game. It's even in the paper. You come up with some dillies, all right. But that's the nuttiest yet! What did you read, the comic pages?"

"I read the Kid Sports Page of *CITY NEWS*."

They were on the patio behind the Walker home. The *CITY NEWS* was on a table. Ron spread the Kid Sports Page on the table.

"Show me," Ron said.

"Right there," Slats said.

Ron read aloud: "The six point win posted by Washington may be misleading. Lincoln played the pre-

season pick as the team to beat in the City League even all the way. Ten times deadlocked, the final tie score was at 29–all. Four free throws by Washington in the final 89 seconds of play decided a very tight game."

He looked at Slats, frowned a little and re-read the summary. Then Ron said: "Look, I phoned the high spots of the game as I saw them. The editor left out most of my very-much-pro-Lincoln stuff, but there is absolutely nothing in the piece about *anybody* losing the game!"

"It says Washington got four points on one-and-one things after I fouled out," Slats muttered.

"It says that Washington got four points on free throws." Ron eyed his tall friend steadily. "There's nothing you could take as even hinting that Durand Stanislaus Salvatore lost the game. What the heck is bugging you?"

Slats shrugged, said nothing. Ron pressed. "C'mon. Give."

"I heard some kids saying I lost the game," Slats said.

"What kids? When?"

"I don't know what kids. After the game."

"Basketball guys? Maybe Butch Arnold? Or Thor Olson, griping because Coach played you in his spot?"

"Huh-uh, nothing like that. Just some kids in the crowd," Slats said quickly.

"I didn't really think Butch or Thor would pull any crazy you-lost-the-game stuff, even though they are great buddies." Ron still frowned. "Migosh," he said, "you do bring up things from 'way out in left field!

There are always big-mouth-know-it-all characters who have to spout! So, you hear some yakheads running their mouths and think the junk they put out means something. Forget it!"

Ron regarded Slats speculatively and his expression cleared. "Speaking of coming up with things: where did that 'jam up the middle' you yelled come from?"

"The basketball book has a section on team defense. No matter whether it is some form of zone defense, a pressing defense or man-for-man defense, it won't work if the other guys have a clear path through the foul lane. The book said to jam up the middle. I guess I was kind of subconsciously thinking of the book and just yelled."

"Well, it sure got Coach's attention." Ron nodded. "You ought to think more about things in the book, looks like. What does it have about rabbit ears?"

"Rabbit ears?"

"Yeah, rabbit ears. Anybody playing in a game can't let himself really *hear* things yelled to get his goat and rattle him. He can't concentrate on his own play if he does. His ears are too big, like a rabbit's. Pay no attention to needling—and that goes for mouth-runners, too!"

CHAPTER TEN

□ *SLATS WONDERS*

RON WALKER brought Slats the newspaper article. The clipping was not from *CITY NEWS*.

"Editor of Kid Sports Page gave it to me," Ron explained. He grinned. "When I phoned in on the Washington game I said Lincoln was a different team when you went in; their defense came to life. Sometimes I sort of get carried away, I guess. I mentioned that Salvatore could be another Hank Monzetti. Anyway, the editor didn't use any of that but he said this article fit right in with what I'd said."

"ALL STATE HIGH SCHOOL STAR IN BIG TWELVE SPOTLIGHT," Slats read, then added, "It's datelined Chicago."

"Yeah. Clipped from a Chicago paper. The office of the Big Twelve Conference commissioner is in Chicago. They keep sports editors well supplied with material promoting publicity for Big Twelve athletics. This piece is about Hank Monzetti. You should get a boost from reading the thing."

Slats read the newspaper clipping.

It has been a long established policy of Big Twelve coaches to develop players slowly. Rarely

79

do first year men attain starting positions. Yet big freshman Hank Monzetti has started every Western State game at center, ranks among the top scorers and leads the Conference in the all-important rebounding category. Monzetti has pulled in rebounds at a rate slightly better than 19 per game.

"My biggest weakness when I came to Western was my shooting," Monzetti told this interviewer. "In junior high and in high school, I was first and last a rebounder. Almost always I was the biggest man in the game.

"But I learned that college ball is different. Things move a lot faster. There are more big men. You have to work harder to out-muscle them. Rebounding is still my primary job, but Western's coaches hammer, hammer, hammer to get me to take the open shot. I was a liability to our offense, but I keep trying and I feel that I have improved."

Slats devoured the article. The final paragraphs especially intrigued him.

Big Hank has his own philosophy of basketball play. "Rebounding is the name of the game," he states flatly. "Get the ball off the board when your team misses a shot and keep putting it up 'til somebody sinks a bucket. Grab the rebound when the other guys miss and get the ball out of there. Hold the other team to one shot. They are not going to beat you if you don't let them score."

Monzetti plays basketball with consuming intensity. He is determined to contribute offensively.

He is getting tip-in baskets; he has developed a hook shot that is deadly from eight to ten feet. He shoots when open after grabbing a rebound; he takes handoffs and drives. He moves around, avoiding overtime-in-the-lane calls and is capable of driving the baseline after he leaves the lane.

On defense the scintillating freshman is absolutely devastating. At times the ferocity of his desire makes it seem that he retains some of the awkwardness he admits to having battled throughout his basketball career. Perhaps Monzetti's only weakness is that he tends to foul heavily. To date he has fouled out more often than he has finished a game.

"I have to work hard all the time to improve my defensive technique," Big Hank says ruefully. "I guess most big fellows have to work to keep from clobbering opponents, and costing their team."

Slats thought of an interview Monzetti gave before a televised Western State game he and Ron had watched. *I've slaved and worked and worked and slaved more so I don't stumble over my own feet,* Monzetti said that day. *Or foul the heck out of guys on the other team.*

Must be he's still slaving and working, Slats thought. If a star like him works to improve defensive techniques, a guy like Salvatore better work even more. There ought to be tips on defensive techniques in the basketball book.

The section in the book headed Techniques of Individual Defense started with what Slats thought an odd statement: A good offense is the best defense. The book went on to qualify the opening sentence.

Coaches who support this thesis cite the indisputable fact that the team with the highest score at the end of a game wins. So, they emphasize offense. But how much good is a flashy offense that produces 80, 90, 100 points, if a porous defense allows the opponents to score 81, 91, 101 points? To win consistently your team must be able to hold down the other team's scoring. And no matter how you spell it, limiting the opponents to as few scoring opportunities as possible is defense.

You have to get out and work to acquire defensive skills. An ability to stick to your opponent like adhesive tape, agility developed through practice and hang-in-there toughness are the marks of a top defensive player.

Slats read on. . . . Work to maintain a stance that gives you balance to change direction with the offensive man's moves . . . . develop your footwork . . . . talk to your opponent. Yell at him when he is about to shoot, pass or dribble . . . . harass him. Some players hear everything and can be thrown off stride. . . .

Slats drew in a breath and let it out. No wonder Hank Monzetti had to work hard to improve. Well, Ron Walker could help Salvatore work on defensive techniques.

"You mean a one-on-one deal?" Ron asked. "Migosh, you won't get much practice going against me. I told you I'm no good at dribbling or shooting—or anything else in this round-ball business!"

"C'mon, Ron! Dribble like you were going to drive in for a layup!"

Ron took the ball at the edge of the driveway, ten feet or so beyond the free throw circle. He began his dribble. He had not been fooling when he said he was no good at dribbling. He bounced the ball too high, and had to keep his eyes riveted on the leather sphere to keep from bumbling it away.

Slats stood with feet wide spread, arms out, half crouched ready to move to either side. Ron slanted to his right. Slats shifted using the boxer's shuffling step as described in the book. Ron took his eyes from the ball when Slats slid in front of him. Ron grabbed at the ball, fumbled it, recovered and started to dribble again, then stopped.

"Broken dribble," he said disgustedly. "It would be your team's ball out of bounds. Nice work."

Slats grunted. He knew his shifting had been ragged and too slow. A good dribbler would have cut back and around him before he could have recovered. He said, "Let's do it again. If you think you can't get past me, shoot. I want to see if I can be ready to block a shot like the book says."

Ron started again from as far back as the concrete drive permitted. He tried a head fake, grabbed the ball at the top of a too-high dribble bounce and lifted the ball in one hand to try a push shot.

"Harraaghgh!"

The sudden, rasping shout from Slats startled Ron. The attempted push shot was wide and much too short. "Migosh, what are you trying to do," he complained. "You scared the pants off me!"

"The book says to harass your man. Talk to him. Yell at him when he's about to shoot." Slats grinned. "Some guys hear everything and can be rattled. Rabbit ears, they call it!"

"Yeah. Where have I heard that before?"

They continued the one-on-one play. Slats knew he was not really getting much practice. He also knew that he fouled Ron too often.

The thing to do was to ask Coach Long to give him help on defensive play, extra work.

Coach Long made it unnecessary for Slats to ask for work on defense. The Lincoln mentor called his squad together during the first practice following the Washington game.

"Basketball is a game of adjustments," the coach began. "We adjusted well to hold Washington's big scorer in check. We did not fast break because they were too big and controlled the boards most of the game. I firmly believe that we will take them when they play in our gym. In the meantime, we meet Wilson Junior High this week on our floor and Roosevelt in their gym before Washington comes here for the start of the second round of our City League schedule."

He stopped and flicked his gaze over the group.

"We made glaring mistakes," Long went on after a time. "Most of them were lapses on defense. We are going to work more on individual defensive play and try to put everything together to improve our total team defense."

Slats was amazed at how closely coaching tips from Coach Long matched advice from the basketball book. But why not? The book's author had coached basketball more than twenty years.

"Guard, center or forward," Coach Long said, "every man plays defense when the other team has possession of the ball. . . . In order to play defense without fouling excessively, keep the man you are guarding in front. . . . Vary your defensive technique. Guard aggressively part of the time, crowd him as much as you can without fouling. Then try sagging away. . . . Anything you can do to make him uncertain will help make the offensive man easier to guard.

"Yell at him, talk to him. . . . Holler out, 'I've got him' and point at him. . . . Your teammates will know you are covering him and he may be disconcerted . . ."

Coach Long gave the ball to Pete Thrall. "You've just taken a pass," the coach said. "Dribble downcourt. Salvatore, guard him. All right, go!"

Thrall was Lincoln's cleverest dribbler. Slats eyed him closely. Thrall changed directions. Slats shifted. He did not shift quickly enough; Thrall was a half-step past when Slats flung out a long arm. His hand slapped Thrall's wrist. Long shrilled his whistle.

"Foul! You run alongside the dribbler if he gets past. Bat the ball loose if you can. But any contact you make will draw a foul call from the official."

"How's a feller gonna guard a dribbler, then?" Bewilderment filled his tone as Slats looked at the coach. "How can you knock the ball away without touching him?"

"It is not easy. You harass him, crowd him as close as you can without blocking him. You make a cut at the ball just as it bounces off the floor—with your outside hand, the one away from the dribbler. Officials just naturally call a foul when the hand nearest the dribbler is used. It is practically impossible to use the inside arm without making contact.

"The undercut at the ball must be timed right, and it requires a great deal of practice to perform. But it can be done, must be done if you are to become a *good* defensive man. Once you have broken the dribble, you may be able to gain possession of the ball. Or it may roll to a teammate. The least that can happen is still to your advantage because you have spoiled the dribbler's drive.

"Try it again."

Try it again. The words echoed in Slats' head after a while. He was sure that Coach worked him more often in the drill and longer than other boys. That was okay, if he could finally get so he did not foul so often.

Slats wondered if such a time would ever come.

CHAPTER ELEVEN

□ *TWO WINS*

SLATS WAS sure he recognized the headline across the sheet of newspaper that Coach Long took from a pocket and unfolded. CITY JUNIOR HIGH LEAGUE DEADLOCKED AFTER THIS WEEK? Why would Coach bring yesterday's Kid Sports Page to the pre-game talk before Lincoln went out to meet Wilson in the first home game?

"Unfortunately, I assume you have all read this stuff," Coach Long began as he inclined his head toward the newspaper.

"Lincoln must be rated an overwhelming favorite to even its league standing at one–one. Coach Long has consistently produced well-coached, disciplined teams and the boys wearing Lincoln's Green and Gold this year measure up to recent Long teams. Unfortunately, Wilson's situation is entirely different.

Three boys counted on at Wilson as a nucleus for this year have moved from the Wilson district. There are no ninth grade boys on the Wilson Junior High squad, and seventh and eighth graders are rarely as big and tall. Lack of size and inexperience will handicap Wilson."

Coach Long folded the Kid Sports Page. He did not speak for a space of time that seemed to stretch endlessly. The coach definitely held Slats Salvatore's gaze, finally said mildly, "The whole piece reads as though it could have been written by our demon sports writer. Happen that your buddy showed it to you, Salvatore?"

Slats shook his head. He frowned. If Ron Walker had written something that got printed, he would for sure have been around bragging.

"That was hardly fair," Coach Long said. "Overlook it, please. I am not unappreciative of the Coach-Long-has-consistently-produced-well-coached-teams. I would say it is a little on the extravagant side. I hope the assessment that you fellows measure up to previous Lincoln teams is accurate. What I strenuously object to is the overwhelming-favorite business.

"I have used up time we usually take to point up our game plan to emphasize two important items. One: team games are won because one team *plays* better that game. Talk of something that happened last week, last year, or whatever seldom influences the outcome of any given game. Two: making one team a favorite because of one, two, or three players is wrong. Basketball is a team game. No one player, or two players win or lose a game. Perhaps I should add a third item; a team lulled into overconfidence is a team headed for the short end when the game is over. All right, everybody out there with just one thing in mind; keep playing the best basketball you know how to play."

Coach Long talked to Slats before the game began. "You're starting in Olson's spot, Salvatore. After the tip-off, drop back to guard. Arnold will play center on offense." The coach hesitated briefly, shook his head, then went on. "You do present a problem," he said. "I certainly don't want to discourage aggressiveness. On the other hand, excessive fouling contributes nothing to the overall team effort. Try not to foul."

Slats tried. But he was called for charging before a minute of play passed. The first quarter was barely half played when he garnered a second personal foul for holding while going after a rebound. Coach Long sent Olson into the game. Slats came to the sideline bewildered. "I just grabbed for the ball," he said.

"But you held down the Wilson boy with one hand!"

The Kid Sports Page was quite evidently in error about seventh and eighth graders not being big—or else Wilson's coach had located a tall ninth grader. Wilson's one big boy consistently rebounded to confound Lincoln. He gave his team more than one try at the Lincoln basket several times by grabbing rebounds off his offensive board. More often than not he limited Lincoln to one shot by out-rebounding Lincoln boys off their board.

Coach Long sent Slats into the game to start the second quarter. Wilson's control of both boards changed. Midpoint of the period Slats out-reached the Wilson big man cleanly going after a rebound off the Wilson board. He tipped the ball to Kraft. A quick pass to Jenkins caught a guard in a two-on-one situation. Kraft faked a drive when Jenkins passed back and the guard had to commit himself. Thrall took Jenkins' sharp pass and scored.

A minute later Slats again grabbed a rebound and made a fast outlet pass to Arnold. Arnold dribbled hard across the center line, seemed set on driving all the way. A guard came out after him, leaving Jenkins open. Arnold bounce-passed around the guard. Jenkins pushed a jumper from the foul circle and the ball swished through the netting.

Lincoln, 14; Wilson, 8. Wilson called a timeout.

"Now you look like a team that knows working together is the name of the game," Coach Long told his boys as they gathered in front of the bench. "Let's keep that old go-go-go! Salvatore, you used your height nicely. Keep it up! Watch the fouls, you have two!"

Slats felt wonderful.

Eighteen seconds after play resumed, he felt a lot less than wonderful. Intent on getting a rebound, Slats pushed off, although he was out-positioned. Three personals. Then five seconds before the end of the period, Slats committed his fourth foul—a holding call when he used his inside arm in trying to snake the ball from a dribbler. He chewed himself out silently.

Even a big, awkward stupe ought to get it through his thick skull that going after a guy who had out-smarted him would bring about a foul call.

Slats Salvatore did not start the second half.

He sat on the bench throughout the third quarter.

Gloom held him completely. He would not get into the game again. The chances of Coach *ever* putting him in a game again were mighty slim. Why should he put a clumsy lug in there who couldn't play without fouling?

The final period ground away. Lincoln's comfortable twelve-point lead seemed more and more to make valid the Kid Sports Page assessment of Wilson's handicaps. Then things happened. Maybe Lincoln's defense unconsciously let down; maybe Lady Luck suddenly decided to smile exclusively on the visiting boys. Whatever it was, it changed the scoreboard figures. Wilson's big boy tipped in two follow-ins and his long lead-out pass after grabbing a rebound off the Lincoln board eluded Olson. A Wilson forward took the ball and dribbled twice, then cashed a driving layup. Lincoln, 28; Wilson, 22.

Olson passed in from beneath the basket and Arnold fumbled the ball enough that the referee called traveling. Wilson out of bounds. Their big center took a pass in the free throw circle and hooked a good shot over Butch Arnold's leap, and Arnold charged into him after the ball left his hands. The Wilson boy swished the ball through the netting on his free throw try.

Lincoln, 28; Wilson, 25.

Coach Long signaled for a timeout. The Lincoln boys came to the sideline to find a grim-faced coach.

"You fellows have short memories," Long said. "I warned you that a team lulled into overconfidence is headed for the short end. Maybe you thought I just talked to fill in the time! Right now you are headed for a big fat fall!"

He let his words sink in for a while. Then Lincoln's coach said, "You fellows have any idea that Wilson boys believed the Kid Sports Page and all you have to do is stand around, you *should* lose! Salvatore replace Olson. All of you get out there and play basketball!"

Slats was in the game exactly 42 seconds.

He out-reached the big Wilson boy and grabbed the rebound from a missed Wilson shot. He zipped the outlet pass to Butch Arnold. Arnold aimed a pass for Bob Jenkins but the ball was intercepted, and the interceptor broke into the open for a twenty-foot jumper. The ball hit the basket rim and bounced high.

Slats drove all out for the rebound; the big Wilson boy drove all out for the rebound. It was probable that neither boy consciously realized that his free hand jammed into his opponent and pushed hard.

Whistles of both officials blasted in unison. Each raised a fisted hand to indicate a foul. One official pointed at Slats; the other official pointed at the Wilson star. Double foul. Everyone in the gymnasium knew it was a fair call.

The Wilson boy dropped the ball through the hoop; Slats lofted the ball gently, it hit the rim and rolled out. Lincoln, 28; Wilson, 26.

And Slats had fouled out.

The final thirty-seven seconds was junior high basketball at its wildest. Neither team could work the ball in for a good shot, the ball was out-of-bounds, or being tossed for jump ball most of the time. The score was unchanged at the final buzzer.

Slats thought about Ron Walker's "rabbit-ears" as

he walked head down toward the locker room. But he could not help hearing comments that came from Lincoln youngsters trooping from the bleachers toward the exit.

"I thought they were supposed to be easy for our guys! . . . Boy, that was close enough! . . . Yeah. The home floor advantage doesn't mean much when the other guys are going to the free throw line every time you look up! . . . That Salvatore! He's so— Sh-h-h! He's right ahead of us! So, maybe he ought to know! . . ."

In the locker room Butch Arnold wiped his sweat-shiny face, then threw the towel against his locker. "Boy, were we lousy! We had a lock on those guys, then nearly let 'em loose!"

He might as well say I nearly let 'em loose, Slats thought. He was about as low in spirit as the shower room drain. He showered and dressed quickly and left the gymnasium. Outside, Ron Walker swung in beside him. Slats eyed his friend morosely.

"Just skip talking about *anything!*" Slats said.

Slats was surprised that Coach Long did not "read him off" during practice sessions before the Roosevelt game. The few times the coach said anything directly to him was more praise than criticism. Somehow the treatment did nothing to restore Salvatore's confidence. He was really surprised when he read the list of starters Coach Long posted for the Roosevelt game.

Salvatore was starting at center for Lincoln.

"Snap out of it," Ron Walker advised the morning of the game. "Roosevelt is not—"

"—as strong as usual," Slats interrupted. "Quote from your sports page: Lincoln should win handily and keep pace with Washington, highly favored over Wilson. Unquote."

Slats drew in a breath, then let it out slowly and added, "You should have put something in about if Salvatore doesn't give Roosevelt the ball and points by fouling all the time!"

"Hey, what do you mean, I should have put in? What I do mostly is phone in the results after games. The dope about who should beat who and why comes from the Kid Sports editor!"

"Well, he better take a look at how many times the other guys have gained from Salvatore's fouling!"

The fourth foul was called on Salvatore three minutes and twelve seconds into the second quarter. Even though officials had not called them, Slats knew that he had made fouls on at least two other occasions. His fourth foul set up one-and-one free throw situations for Roosevelt.

The boys wearing Roosevelt Blue and White gave their home fans something to cheer about by counting six points from the free throw line before the timer's horn sounded the end of the first half. Score: 19–19.

Slats sat on the bench at the start of the third quarter. He was still there when the fourth period got under way. I'll be here the rest of the game, he thought gloomily. Coach doesn't dare risk playing me more. But midway of the final period of play, Coach Long clutched Slats' arm.

"They've assigned one man to screen Arnold out," the coach said. "They're grabbing most of the rebounds from both boards. Go in for Olson. Try to stay away from fouling, we need your height."

Slats tried. He snared two rebounds from Lincoln's board and one of them resulted in a basket. He grabbed the ball three times off the Roosevelt backboard.

Butch Arnold tipped a missed shot through the netting. Roosevelt passed upfloor and fired a jump shot from sidecourt. It missed. Slats took the rebound and sizzled a perfect outlet pass to Thrall. Thrall and Jenkins broke fast and the two-on-one setup paid off with Thrall's layup. 31–25, Lincoln.

In a melee after Pete Jenkins rimmed a twenty-foot jumper, Slats tipped the ball over the orange ring and after a Roosevelt boy hurried a shot and missed, Slats grabbed the rebound, flipped the outlet pass to Butch Arnold and the Arnold-Thrall-Jenkins fast break overwhelmed two defenders and Thrall dunked another layup. Lincoln, 35; Roosevelt, 25.

Roosevelt called a timeout. "You can't afford to ease off," Coach Long said.

When play resumed Roosevelt's best defensive player shifted to guarding Slats. The Roosevelt boy was not really tall, but he was quick and clever. He outmaneuvered Slats and grabbed a rebound. He used a fine head fake and cut the opposite way. Slats flung out a long arm—after the excellent move had him beaten. Whistles of both officials sounded. There were moans from the Lincoln section.

It seemed that every time Slats fouled in a crucial spot, his team suffered by being put into the one-and-one situation. Their ten-point lead began to dissipate after Slats fouled out.

A tip-in after a missed long shot brought the score to Lincoln, 36; Roosevelt, 35 as the clock registered four seconds left to play. The throw-in came to Thrall. Two dribbles, a quick pass to Jenkins. Three dribbles, pass back to Thrall. Dribble—the timer's signal ended the game.

Slats wondered if he deliberately went past Lincoln people in order to hear what they were saying. He heard.

"Another few seconds, man, and we would'a been sunk! . . . They sure finished strong! . . . Strong? Man, they had us on the ropes! . . . That Salvatore! . . . Yeah, Coach Long plays that clown, he gives the other guys ten or twelve points besides possession of the ball a lot of times! . . . Hey, wait a sec! We weren't going so hot until Salvatore came back in the game! . . . So, say he made a couple of baskets—one, actually, I think! . . . Yeah, one. O-N-E! He gave them a lot more points than he counted for us!"

CHAPTER TWELVE

□ *MAYBE—JUST MAYBE*

RON WALKER swallowed the last bit of golden roll-cake, licked the thumb and forefinger that had held the delicacy and eyed Slats. Disbelief, wariness, then questioning followed each other in Ron's expression and finally reluctant acceptance.

"You mean it!" Ron's tone came close to expressing horror. "Migosh! You can't turn in your basketball gear. The free throw competition is next week. You're head man on the chart!"

"And how much does that mean? I missed a free throw in the Wilson game when the pressure was on!"

"Nobody ever made *every* shot! You're going to represent Lincoln, man!"

"Mike Kazerski will probably do a better job than I would."

"Okay, say you brush the free throw competition under the rug, the team needs you. Migosh! Coach started you against Roosevelt!"

"Yeah." Slats lifted his shoulders, then let them droop. "And he knows now that Salvatore hurts the team more than he helps. Everybody knows!"

"That's crazy! What do you mean?"

Slats repeated things he had heard Lincoln students say after the game. "And don't give me any 'rabbit ears' stuff."

Ron stared, apparently at a loss for words for once. Slats wondered what comeback the kid sportswriter would dream up. But before Ron said anything, Mrs. Salvatore came through the arch between dining area and kitchen in the Salvatore home.

It was plain that Slats Salvatore must have inherited some of his height from his mother. She was tall and big-boned. She was wiping her hands on her apron, then she tucked a wayward strand of very black hair behind an ear as she smiled at Ron.

"You like these roll-cakes?" she said.

"Do I ever!" There could not have been more sincerity in Ron's tone. "They're super-super!"

"Maybe this Coach you and Durand talk of would like my roll-cakes?"

Ron flicked a quick glance at Slats. "Coach Long would—"

"Mom!" Slats interrupted. "I don't think—that is, I mean, sure, Coach would like them. But if I took him roll-cakes it would look as though I was trying to—to—well, you just have to understand that—"

"Now you know I bake my cakes so people will enjoy them. And your coach, he is always so busy—he probably never gets to eat good cakes. You tell him to stop by here and I will give him some."

"But Mom!" Slats groaned.

"Always I make my roll cakes Monday morning," Mrs. Salvatore continued, ignoring Slats. "I will make an extra batch this time. Ask this coach to be with you and we will talk."

The telephone rang. Ludmilla Nada Salvatore went to the kitchen to answer it. To her, everything was settled. Coach Long would come over to have roll-cakes and talk. Slats stared at Ron and frowned.

"How about that?" Ron said. "It's for sure you can't pass your mom's invitation on to Coach and then hand in your equipment!"

"You're talking like a monkey out of his tree! I'm not passing any invitation on to Coach!"

"Okay, so *I'll* pass it on! When your mom said 'Ask this coach to be with you,' she was looking at both of us." Ron pushed his glasses higher on his nose and grinned.

"Ron, you can't do it. What would the coach think? What would the other kids say? There is such a thing as—as—"

"Loyalty, you're maybe trying to say? Or keeping faith with a friend?"

Ron stopped and eyed Slats a moment, then went on. "You use that as a lever on me, it has to be okay to apply leverage on you. I'll be loyal and lay off inviting the coach—you keep faith with the team and lay off crazy thinking about handing in your basketball gear!"

"What'd your mom say when you explained that Coach won't be coming to sample her roll-cakes?"

Ron asked the question as he and Slats came from the classroom session of Physical Ed. Coach-teacher Long always held the class on Monday. He attended the weekly meeting of Lincoln teachers that day and did not want his basketball team to change to basketball gear until 45 minutes after the final class hour.

"I haven't told her," Slats said gloomily. "I've been trying to think of a way without hurting her, or lying. Every time I started leading up to it, Mom had something to say about how I should let her help and she just wants to talk to Coach—and—blame it, I wish I'd never had you look up her name's meaning!"

"Migosh, she'll be expecting Long! You gotta tear home right now and tell her before you have to go to practice!"

"Uh-huh, just like that!" Slats snorted. "I tell you, I've *tried* to explain that he won't be—" He stopped and clutched Ron's arm. "You explain! She'll listen to you—I hope!"

A school custodian was at the bicycle rack. He was reading off a boy who had not locked his bicycle. "—then it gets stolen and the kid and his folks land on us like a—" The custodian broke off as Slats wheeled his bike from the rack. Ron was already astride his. The man barked, "Where do you kids think you're going?"

"Why, we thought we'd ride our bikes home," Ron said.

"Just a ding-dang minute! How come you can wheel out so fast? You don't lock your bikes?"

Ron pointed at the long-hasp lock Slats was snapping shut around the springs of his bike saddle, then pointed to the lock fastened beneath his own saddle.

"Ship-shape and accounted for," Ron said. "You

have a combination lock, you leave the dial a couple of spaces off the key number. Turn it back when you want to unlock—open sesame!" He waved a hand airily. "You're unlocked, snapped on and away in nothing flat like a magician!"

"Smart-alecky type, eh?" The custodian scowled. "You might about as well not lock it at all. Other kids know about combination locks. The wrong one wants your bike, all he does is move the dial and—say, how do I know you two aren't wrong ones? What's your names?"

Slats told him. Ron saw that he had rubbed the man the wrong way. He told his name, then added, "Look, I didn't mean to sound smart-alecky. I'm sorry. I—"

"Ron Walker, eh? Whose homeroom are you in?"

"We're both in Ninth Grade 2. Look, we're in a hurry. Can't you—"

"Hold it right where you are until I check!"

The custodian started for the back entrance near the bicycle racks. He would use the building phone and call the principal's office. Ron kicked disgustedly at the bicycle rack.

"Me and my big mouth!" He grimaced at Slats. "Somebody must have leaned on him pretty hard and made him extra touchy. But it's me on the griddle. You go on and tell your mom. He probably won't say anything if one of us is here when he gets—"

"So it'll be me here," Slats cut in. "I told you I've tried to explain to Mom. You go on. The guy might not get back very soon, but he'll surely make it so I make practice on time."

The custodian was gone more than a half-hour. It seemed like an hour and a half to Slats. Slats said quickly, "We did have something important to do, sir. I hope it's okay that one of us went on to take care of it."

"Okay," the man said gruffly. "You're in the clear from the office. But I still say you ought not to leave your bikes locked like the other kid said."

"Yes, sir." Slats nodded agreement, repeated, "yes, sir. It's all right if I go on to basketball practice, sir?"

"I said you was in the clear."

Coach Long pointed out mistakes made in the game Friday, mentioned outstanding play of boys who had earned it. "We play basketball in spurts," he finished. "Then we mill around as though we don't know how the game is played. We go against Kennedy this week. They'll murder us if we let up like we've been doing. All right, we'll scrimmage."

He called off a starting five to be the varsity and five boys to take off their shirts to oppose the first team. Slats was at center for the Skins.

From the first center jump of the scrimmage, Slats Salvatore and Butch Arnold carried on a continuing battle. Coach Long called one or the other time and again for fouling—charging, holding, pushing-off, what have you. It was not long before Arnold was glaring at Salvatore and Slats was not exactly returning smiles of sweetness and light.

Coach Long shrilled the practice to an end after shorter play than usual.

"That'll do it, for today," he said. "Arnold and Salvatore, come to my office before you shower."

Coach Long indicated a chair when Slats came in. The chair was opposite a half-open door to a room beyond the office. Gym pads were arranged on the floor in a twenty-foot square. Slats noted the set of boxing gloves hanging by their laces from the door knob.

Butch Arnold came minutes after Slats had taken a chair. Arnold saw the gloves, looked from them to Slats and back to the boxing gloves. Then suddenly Arnold looked wide-eyed at the coach.

"The mats and gloves are ready," Coach Long said. "That's the way things are. This nutty business is going to be settled here, today. I am more than a little weary of an Arnold-Salvatore feud ruining the development of our basketball team."

"Feud!" The word burst from Butch Arnold. "Golly, Coach, what do you mean? I don't have any feud with—"

"You don't really expect me to buy that." The coach's words were a quiet statement that cut through Arnold's protest. Long turned toward Slats Salvatore. "When I did my practice teaching in college," he said, "a situation came about that involved nit-picking, half-serious and half-because-they-didn't-realize-what-they-were-doing-to-a-team. My teacher—the team coach—handled it by putting the gloves on the pair and setting them at each other until they reached a common understanding. Arnold is well aware that I have established the custom here at Lincoln."

Arnold looked at Salvatore; Slats looked at Butch Arnold and wondered if the other big boy felt as uncomfortable as he did.

"Either of you have anything to say before we go into the other room?" Long asked.

"Golly, Coach, I—" Butch Arnold broke off and flicked a glance at Slats, then went on. "I don't want to fight, but I'm not afraid to!"

"Salvatore?"

"Yes, sir."

"Does that mean you have something to say?"

"No, sir. That is, I—" Slats gulped. "Well, a fellow don't go for being chewed on because he—he—well, darn it, I know I nearly lost the game. But—"

"When did I chew on you?" Butch Arnold interrupted. "Just tell me when I chewed on you!"

Slats looked at him. "In the locker room after the Wilson game," Slats said. He quoted: "Boy, were we lousy! We had a lock on those guys, then nearly let 'em loose! That 'we' meant Slats Salvatore!"

Butch Arnold frowned, then abruptly his expression cleared.

"Golly, it was a guy named Arnold was to blame for Wilson getting close! Remember, I juggled a pass-in and traveled, gave them the ball and then charged their guy after he hooked a shot over me? He made the free throw and those three points brought them to only three points behind. You could say it was my fault you fouled out, too.

"Your outlet pass was perfect, but the lousy pitch I aimed at Jenkins was intercepted and the guy who intercepted got open for a jumper and it was the rebound from his missed shot that you fouled out on. There shouldn't have *been* a Wilson shot to rebound!"

Butch Arnold shook his head.

"Boy, when I said 'we were lousy' it should for sure have been 'Arnold was lousy'! You gotta believe I wasn't chewing you out, or anybody else but me!"

Slats believed him. He sat there and wondered what to do or say. Finally he swallowed dryly and said, "Well, all the times we've tangled, I guess it's been me much as you. But I never did try to get rough to get even, or anything."

Butch Arnold moved uncomfortably. "I'd better not say me, too," he said. "Some of the times I elbowed or slammed a hip into you, I figured to get even for something you'd done to me."

A space of time passed by with neither boy speaking. Coach Long finally said, "You fellows seem to have cleared things up some."

The boys eyed each other and grinned. They said nothing, but the grins spoke volumes.

"All right." Coach Long nodded. "I had a feeling that talking things over might do it, but I wasn't sure. Looks as though we won't need the gloves. Go get your shower, Arnold. Hang on a bit, will you, Salvatore?"

After Butch Arnold was gone, the coach eyed Slats for a moment, and then said, "You've heard of Hank Monzetti?"

"You mean the basketball star?" Slats' expression

mirrored his surprise. Coach Long nodded. "Sure, I saw him on T.V. And Ron Walker gave me a clipping about Monzetti being one of the top scorers in the conference. There was quite a lot about him working so hard to—"

Slats broke off abruptly and gave the coach a keen look. He was suddenly sure he knew why Coach brought up Hank Monzetti.

"—improve his defensive technique." Long finished the sentence Slats had broken off. "He guessed that most big fellows have to work hard to keep from clobbering opponents."

He inclined his head, then went on. "Yes, I have the same clipping. Hank sends them to me. I'm as proud of the clippings as Hank. You see, Hank Monzetti was in junior high where I earned a practice teaching credit by assisting the basketball coach. You remind me a great deal of Hank Monzetti at that stage."

"Was Monzetti one of the guys the coach had put on boxing gloves?"

"No." Long's eyes twinkled. "But besides being big, Hank's confidence in himself got so shaky that he talked with me about turning in his equipment." The twinkle was gone as the coach eyed Slats steadily and added, "He thought he hurt the team more than he helped."

Slats frowned. Those were almost exactly the words he had said to Ron Walker. He said, "Ron Walker has been talking with you!"

"You are very fortunate to have a staunch booster like Walker," the coach said. "Yes, Walker brought out some things about Salvatore that I probably should have known. You are not the smooth player you can become, any more than Monzetti was a finished star in his junior high days.

"But you have progressed more than you give yourself credit for. To allow the remarks of some irresponsible youngsters to upset you to the point of dropping basketball is ridiculous. You have heard no criticism from teammates and you can be sure that you would not be playing if I did not think that you help us."

Slats said half to himself, "Ron had to be here today."

"He was." Long inclined his head. "Walker brought me two of the most delicious pastries I have ever eaten. Compliments of your mother. Please tell her for me how much I enjoyed the treat. I look forward to meeting Mrs. Salvatore at our next PTA meeting."

Ron was astraddle his bike when Slats came around the corner of the building to the gymnasium bicycle rack. He eyed Slats, nodded, drew in a breath and said,

"I figured he would tell you I took him a couple of roll-cakes. Okay, so he gave me an opening and I unloaded how your crazy idea of quitting and your mom's roll-cakes extra batch were all tangled together.

"Before you jump down my throat, let me tell you that I had to take the roll-cakes to Coach in order to keep your mother from doing it herself. She may not know a basketball field goal from a football score, but she's no dummy when it comes to knowing things aren't so hot right now with you and basketball! She wanted to tell the coach not to let her Durand quit cause you'd be good for basketball and you were trying hard—boy, did I have a time with her!"

Ron shook his head, then brushed his hair back from his forehead.

"So, I told her I would tell the coach and I did. Coach promised that he would back me up in what I told her, if she asked him. So I told your mom that coaching was a profession, like medicine, and that coach didn't call at people's house and was always so busy that people did not go to see him except in emergencies. Then I had to talk a mile a minute to convince her this was not an emergency!"

Ron pushed his glasses higher on his nose and said, "Okay, now you can let me have it!"

Slats regarded the small boy, shook his head, then squeezed Ron's shoulder. "You're really something," Slats said. "If I work hard at it, maybe I'll get so I appreciate you—just maybe!"

CHAPTER THIRTEEN

□ A WIN AND A LOSS

ANY THOUGHT of turning in his basketball gear was blotted from Slats Salvatore's mind. He read and re-read the newspaper clipping about Hank Monzetti. He felt almost a kinship to the Western State star.

Monzetti and Salvatore; both big guys, both learning basketball from Coach Long. Monzetti and Salvatore: both discouraged and ready to quit, both given new determination from Coach Long. Things that Coach had said stuck in Slats' mind.

". . . . far from the smooth player you can become . . . . progressed more than you give yourself credit for . . . . you would not be playing if I did not think you help us. . . ."

He thought of Ron Walker's words the day they had seen Monzetti on television. . . . "You could be Lincoln Junior High School's Hank Monzetti." . . . Just maybe Slats Salvatore *could* be Lincoln's Monzetti and help win the City Junior High championship.

Just maybe.

Well, Salvatore, it's up to you!

He hurried through his chores and the evening meal every day so he could get in as much practice as possible. He tried shots at the basket from different spots in the free throw lane after dodging imaginary guards. He out-maneuvered make-believe opponents to go up after rebounds. He practiced tipping the ball into the metal hoop after missed shots. He worked and slaved and worked and slaved at shooting hook shots from the pivot position eight to ten feet up the lane from the basket.

Coach Long never made a coaching tip to anybody that Slats Salvatore did not take as aimed at him. He worked on those tips during practice and he worked hard on them in his own private basket area—courtesy of Ron Walker.

And always he shot free throws, at the gym and in the Walker driveway. The free throw competition coming up was never out of the back of his thoughts.

"I don't know," Slats said to Ron the day of the Lincoln-Kennedy game. "Just when I begin to think I may be getting a teeny bit nearer to being a basketball player—whammo! I do some stupid thing like pushing off when a guy has me beaten, and there goes another foul!"

"No use saying you don't foul." Ron nodded agreement. "But you *are* improving. You get fouled a lot, too, and anytime you're on that free throw line points for Lincoln are probably coming up. You're rippling that old net with tip-ins and hook shots. Now, you're scoring a lot more points than your fouls give the other guys!"

Ron eyed his tall pal. Slats still looked far from happy. Ron said, "Look, I watched the game-type scrimmage yesterday. You were in there grabbing rebounds and scoring and—"

"—I fouled out with half the fourth period left to play," Slats finished.

"You used to foul out with half the *second* quarter left—or sometimes half the first! Say that you foul more than you like; call it too much. Lincoln is still a better team on both defense and offense with you in there. One of these days you'll get things together, and you'll hang it on the other guys all the way."

Slats did not "hang it on the other guys all the

way." But he did get things together for more than three quarters. The Kennedy center—their big man who had wrecked Washington—counted only one goal from the field the first half. Slats beat him 5–3 grabbing rebounds, and dropped two hook shots through the cords. A Salvatore tip-in of a missed Pete Thrall jumper just before the end of the first half gave Lincoln a 19–17 edge on the scoreboard.

During the third quarter Slats dropped a hook shot, a tip-in and two free throws through the basket. But he also committed the final foul he could and still remain in the game. Then in the first minute of the fourth quarter, Slats was fouled while hooking a shot and the basket was good. He dropped the free throw through the netted hoop. The three-point play raised Lincoln's lead to 31–26.

A Kennedy boy threw the inbounds pass long to a teammate near the time line. Lincoln's defense was caught lagging; the receiver of the pass should have driven in for a layup, but he hurried a jump shot from the free-throw circle. The ball hit the basket rim and bounced high.

Slats was a step behind the big Kennedy center; the other boy had Slats beaten. But it was Slats who clutched the ball and came down with the rebound. Shrill blasts came from the whistles of both officials.

"Salvatore, pushing off!"

Slats Salvatore was out of the game.

Scoreboard figures registered Lincoln, 37; Kennedy, 34 at the timer's final buzzer. Salvatore's three-point play provided Lincoln's winning margin. But Slats would have been immeasureably happier if his fouling had not given Kennedy impetus.

Would he ever finish a game without fouling out?

CHAPTER FOURTEEN

☐ FREE THROW

> Yea-a-a, Slats! Yea-a-a, Salvatore!
> They all make some
> But Slats makes more!
>
> Yea-a-a, Slats! Yea-a-a, Salvatore!
> They all make some
> But Slats makes more!

Cheerleaders swayed in rhythmic accord with the chant from the Lincoln Junior High section in Municipal Auditorium. They had yelled the traditional Yea-a-a, Lincoln! Yea, Salvatore! FIGHT cheer before the free throw competition began. After Slats won his first round by making twenty-four of twenty-five tries, Ron Walker and the cheerleaders got together and came up with the chant.

It was new and different and Slats Salvatore was at first almost stunned. The chant seemed to drown out cheers from other sections for their competitors, as far as Slats was concerned.

He won his second round match by sinking twenty-five straight free throws. He stood on the stage and looked out over the jam-packed auditorium. He had expressed doubts to Ron Walker that the Kid Sports Page promotion would amount to much. Now he thought of Ron's reaction.

"You putting me on?" Ron's expression was as incredulous as the tone of his question. "Man, you are eighteen miles and seven hundred yards out of bounds! It'll be a BIG thing! Kids from every junior high in the county and city will be there to yell for their man!"

Ron's prediction hit dead center. Municipal Auditorium was a madhouse of yelling junior high students before the first free throw effort was tossed. Surprisingly the din increased as the steady shooting of Slats Salvatore and the Washington star dropped boys from other schools out of the race. It seemed to Slats that the Lincoln chant grew stronger than the cheers for the boy representing Washington Junior High.

Yea-a-a, Slats! Yea-a-a, Salvatore!
They all make some
But Slats makes more! . . .

Definitely the chant was louder. Something about it must appeal to kids whose school champion was out.

It did not occur to Slats that seeing awkward-appearing, gangle-shanks Salvatore drop free throws through the netted metal ring had more appeal to more youngsters than the smoothness of the Washington star.

The editor of Kid Sports Page came to the microphone standing front-center of the stage. He beckoned

the two finalists to join him, then spoke into the mike.

"Each contestant will shoot blocks of five free throw tries," the editor said, "alternating as to turns. At the completion of five blocks—twenty-five tosses each —the boy with the greater number of successful shots will be awarded a plaque as Champion of City and County Junior High Schools for this year. Should there be a tie after twenty-five shots each, the boys will continue throwing in blocks of five until we have a winner. Salvatore throws the first five."

Slats and the Washington boy grasped hands. His opponent eyed Slats, grinned a little shakily and said, "Might be I *do* wish it was a free throw deal with no opposition, this time. I can't wish you luck, 'cause you *are* all that good!"

Slats frowned. What the heck? Then suddenly he remembered when he went into the Washington-Lincoln game. Almost the same words now as then. Was the guy trying to psych him? Aw, come off it, Salvatore! Slats inclined his head. "Make what you said times two," he said.

Slats bounced the ball several times before toeing the free throw line. He thought about the chant. It was really something to have the kids yelling a cheer made up just for him. Ron must have had a lot to do with that. How about this Washington guy? Was he—all right, knock it off, Salvatore. Concentrate on making free throws good.

His first effort did not even reach the basket.

Slats knew he was more aware of the concerted groan from the Lincoln section than he should have been. Rabbit ears! He gave himself a disgusted chewing out. He forced tense muscles to relax.

Slats Salvatore dropped the next four cleanly through the netting. But the Washington star smoothly dropped five. He started the second round. Again he scored a perfect five. Slats matched the perfect block.

The ball dropped through the basket with monotonous regularity. Slats finished his twenty-five tries with a score of twenty-four made—but the Washington boy finished with twenty-five tries and twenty-five made.

The boys shook hands. A rousing cheer came from Lincoln's section. The varsity basketball squad, standing together, followed Butch Arnold as he led a cheer.

> Yea-a-a, Slats! Yea-a-a, Salvatore!
> You did your best
> Who could ask for more?
> LINCOLN! LINCOLN! LINCOLN!

A great warmness filled Slats. A feeling of being accepted, of belonging, of confidence. A fellow did his best, and nobody put him down!

CHAPTER FIFTEEN

□ *A GOOD MAYBE*

Beat 'em, bust 'em
That's our custom!
Yea-a-a, Team!

WASHINGTON'S CHEER rolled from their side. Lincoln
cheerleaders led Lincoln in an answering yell.

Yea-a-a, Green! Yea-a-a, Gold!
Go-o-o, Green! Go-o-o, Gold!
Yea-a-a, Lincoln!
Go! Go! Go!

Washington sent another yell out.

Give 'em the axe, the axe, the axe!
Give 'em the axe, give 'em the axe!
Give 'em the axe—WHERE?
Right in the neck, the neck, the neck!
Right in the neck, right in the neck
Right in the neck—THERE!
Washington! Washington! Washington!
Fight! Fight! FIGHT!

Cheerleaders leaped and threw arms high and legs
wide at the FIGHT!

On the floor the green-and-gold clad boys all wore sober determined expressions while they warmed up before the start of the second half. Slats glanced at the scoreboard.

Washington, 24; Lincoln, 24.

"Washington is as good as any junior high team around these parts," Coach Long told his squad before they left the locker room for the start of the game. "The only game they've lost bad was to Kennedy at Kennedy. I'm sure it will be a far different result when they play Kennedy at Washington. Their big man leads the league in scoring. We have to hold him down. We must play up to our potential all the way to stay with this team."

During halftime intermission Long simply told his team that nothing had changed. Then he reminded them of a truism that is posted in many team rooms: WHEN THE GOING GETS TOUGH, THE TOUGH GETS GOING.

The timer's horn sounded end of halftime intermission. Players gathered around their coaches. Slats gave himself a pep talk while he gripped hands with teammates and Coach Long.

You've fouled your guy twice, watch it! Arnold and Olson couldn't hold him in the other game. You gotta bear down and not foul out. You can do it! Hey! How about all the confidence? Don't get cocky!

Slats grinned. He knew he was not being cocky. He was just showing strong belief in Slats Salvatore. He wanted to be a Hank Monzetti for Lincoln. Just maybe he could. Lincoln kids yelling for Salvatore even after he lost the free throw competition had done things for him.

Salvatore out-jumped Washington's big star, slanted the tipoff to Butch Arnold. Jenkins raced all out toward the Washington basket. Arnold lobbed a pass that led the Lincoln forward perfectly.

All alone, Jenkins dribbled in and dunked a layup through the cords. Lincoln led 26–24. The margin lasted exactly twenty-one seconds. A Washington boy slipped around Al Kraft, took a sharp pass and pushed a twenty-six foot jumper into the metal ring.

Tie score. Then the lead see-sawed the entire quarter. Scoreboard figures registered Washington, 32; Lincoln, 32 at the timer's horn.

Slats hooked a basket from ten feet in the first twelve seconds of the final period. Washington's inbounds pass was poor. The ball sailed out of bounds across court. Arnold took the throw-in from Kraft, held up three fingers to signal play pattern Number Three. Slats trotted to the high post spot in the free throw circle.

Arnold flipped the ball to Slats and cut for the basket. Jenkins and Thrall maneuvered trying to break free, but guards stuck close. Arnold broke into the clear momentarily, but before Slats saw Arnold's break, the man guarding Slats left him to pick up Arnold.

Slats dribbled once and drove for the basket. He carried the ball high and rolled it off his fingers over the basket rim. Lincoln, 36; Washington, 32.

Washington threw the ball inbounds. A dribble. A sharp pass to their center. Slats knew he was beaten and tried to hold back. But he could not stop his lunge in time. He barged hard into the Washington star as he got off a shot. It was wide, but the foul in the act of shooting gave him two free throws. He dropped both tries cleanly through the netting. Washington, 34; Lincoln, 36.

Then for minutes defenses of both teams stymied the offenses. Two minutes showed on the clock when Slats again fouled his man. Coach Long sent Mike Kazerski into the game to replace Salvatore. Kazerski took Arnold's man, Arnold switched to cover the Washington big man.

This time neither free throw dropped. But in the next thirty-eight seconds, Arnold lost his man twice. A layup basket, then a hook shot from ten feet out slanted through the netted ring.

Washington, 38; Lincoln, 36.

Coach Long signaled a timeout. A minute and twenty-two seconds left to play. "Report back in," Long said to Slats. "Try to keep from fouling!"

Slats only nodded. He could not have squeezed words through the dry tightness of his throat.

Arnold took the throw-in from Thrall. He dribbled across the center line, signaled for play pattern Number Two. Everyone was covered. Arnold passed to Jenkins, coming back. Washington was in a pressing defense. They stuck to Lincoln boys like adhesive tape sticks to a hairy leg.

Butch Arnold was called for a three-seconds-in-the-lane violation. Washington out of bounds. The clock showed fifteen seconds of playing time left. They could pass and dribble and kill the clock. But the receiver of the pass inbounds took a step too many before he started his dribble. Traveling. Lincoln's ball out of bounds.

Thrall threw in to Arnold. Slats had a step on his man as they tore upcourt. Arnold whipped a pass to Slats.

"Shoot! Shoot!" Lincoln people shrieked. "Time is almost up! Shoot!"

Slats drove for the basket. As he started his leap to carry the ball up, he was hammered from behind. The ball dropped short. But whistles shrilled. A two-shot foul.

Slats toed the free throw line, kept his eyes fastened on the basket rim. His long legs bent at the knees and the ball swooped upward. The netting *swished.* A perfect shot rippled through the basket.

An explosion of noise burst from the crowd. Another successful free throw would tie the score. The gym quieted as the referee underhanded the ball to Slats.

"He's a cinch to make it!" The wail from a Washington supporter sounded loud in the quiet. "He sunk a million in that free throw thing last week!"

It never entered Slats' mind that he might miss the second toss. Okay, so if he made it the score was tied. Then what? One more foul would put him out of the game. Arnold had not been able to handle Washington's big man. Slats stepped away from the line. He motioned Butch Arnold. "Call a timeout," Slats said.

On the sideline he spoke hurriedly to Coach Long.

"That guy could ruin us in overtime. How about me banging the ball off the backboard or dropping it so it'll bounce off the iron. Me and Butch go up for a tip-in or bat the ball back to Jenkins or Thrall."

Coach eyed Slats levelly, shook his head. "No," Long said. "I have confidence in you. You need to believe in yourself. Make the free throw. You can handle your man in overtime!"

When time was in, Slats did not fuss around. He toed the line and eyed the basket. He bent his knees and lofted the ball upward.

The shot was a tiny bit too long. The ball hit the brace and back rim of the basket. Slats stood as though petrified. This was awful, much worse than missing that free throw last week.

"Slats! Sink it!"

The yell from Butch Arnold jarred Slats from his momentary freeze. Arnold's leap carried him just high enough that he tipped the rebound away from the Washington center. Slats grabbed the ball. One big step carried him near the basket. He went up smoothly, rolled the sphere off his fingers as he had done so many times at the basket hung from the Walker garage.

The ball dropped gently through the netting. Two points. The reverse three-point play made the score Lincoln, 39; Washington, 38.

Washington threw inbounds from beneath the basket. It was a hurried pass, not too good. The receiver juggled the ball before he started a dribble. Washington rooters yelled for him to shoot. He heaved the ball. The timer's gun sounded. The ball landed far wide of the basket.

Teammates hugged Slats, pounded him on the back. He struggled toward the stairs to the locker room through what seemed the whole Lincoln student body. Suddenly Ron Walker was beside him.

"That does it!" Ron exulted. "We're leading the league! Nobody'll catch us now. Man, this is a BIG win!"

Slats grinned. Whether Lincoln stayed in the lead had to be a maybe. But there was no maybe about this being a big win for Slats Salvatore.